MW00814258

FATE BOOK

a Novel

MIMI JEAN PAMFILOFF

First Edition.

Cover Design by EarthlyCharms.com

Editing by Dina Rubin

Copyright © 2013 by Mimi Jean Pamfiloff

All rights reserved. No part of this publication may be reproduced, distributed, or transmitted in any form or by any means, including photocopying, recording, or other electronic or mechanical methods, without the prior written permission of the writer, except in the case of brief quotations embodied in critical reviews and certain other noncommercial uses permitted by copyright law.

This is a work of fiction. Names, characters, places, brands, media, and incidents are either the product of the author's imagination or are used fictitiously. The author acknowledges the trademarked status and trademark owners of various products referenced in this work of fiction, which have been used without permission. The publication/use of these trademarks are not authorized, associated with, or sponsored by the trademark owners.

ISBN-13:978-1490995939
ISBN-10:1490995935

Dedicated

To

our

GHOSTS

and

Rabbit Holes.

OTHER BEST-SELLING WORK BY MIMI JEAN PAMFILOFF:

The Accidentally Yours Series

Accidentally in Love with…a God?

Accidentally Married to…a Vampire?

Sun God Seeks…Surrogate?

Accidentally…Evil? (a Novella)

Vampires Need Not…Apply? Coming September 2013

Accidentally…Cimil? (a Novella) Coming January 2014

Acknowledgments:

As always, I have to thank my awesome hubby and boys for their support and sacrifices. I couldn't do any of this without them. Love you guys.

Eternal, heartfelt gratitude toward the wonderfully supportive people in my life who took time out of their busy schedules to help make this book something better. Vicki Randall, Karen Schwartz, and Naughty Nana. (And you, too, Ally Kraai!)

Finally, a *big* thanks to my Accidentally Yours fans (woooo!) for inspiring this novel! Your Facebooking with my hunky gods gave me the idea. (If only Votan would come to life and deliver cookies to your doorstep. Right?)

FATE BOOK

PART ONE

Sunny Skies

&

Green Pastures Ahead

CHAPTER ONE

Monday.

"This is your day, Dakota. Yours. And he *will* notice you," I said, repeating my corny affirmation as I gazed confidently into the bathroom mirror and inspected my smooth, red hair one final time. Its glossy sheen was a definite improvement over my usual trademark frizz-fest. That straightening iron was worth every penny; although, it wasn't my penny. My parents had invested a fortune in me lately, including professional teeth whitening after having my braces off, contacts to show off my big blues, a new wardrobe, and a shiny, red, super-fab eighteenth b-day gift.

Oh yeah. I am talking *car*. VW Bug. And it was all mine, mine, mine.

Now, if you're thinking that this is the most spoiled, materialistic girl you've ever met, give me a chance to explain.

Ready? Here it is...

I'm a loser.

Big time.

What defines a loser? Well, I possess a certain lack of self-confidence and an undeniable social awkwardness, along with a love of all things geeky. Example: If I had to choose between watching *Pretty Little Liars* or a special about aliens and Egyptians, ninety-nine percent of the time I'd watch the aliens and DVR *PLL*. But I'd DVR the alien show, too, so I could watch it again. Ten times. I know, kind of geeky.

I'm also terminally unpopular—the bubonic plague's got nothing on me—which is why I've had one and only one friend since the first grade: Mandy Giovanni. Lucky for Mandy, she's not as socially revolting to the general population as I am, but that's because Janice Jensen, head cheerleader, doesn't consider her enemy *numero uno*. That privilege belongs to me. Why? Couldn't tell you. But my hypothesis is that it's like those chickens that gang up on the weakest hen and partake in communal pecking until loser chicken is left with zero feathers. Janice's favorite way to remove my plumage is to tell me I smell like a dog because I work at an animal shelter on weekends, and, apparently, being kind to homeless pets is not cool in her book.

Yes. Janice and her cheer-posse are such peckers. Yes. I mean it both ways.

So that's me. Loser chicken.

Well, I used to be, anyway. Because today, after the weeklong spring break, I would return to school as the new me. Eighteen, flat hair, and confident. All in preparation for an even bigger event: graduation. I absolutely couldn't wait to enter that big, wonderful world waiting just for me. College, new friends, cute boys who might not throw up at the sight of me. Paradise. I've waited years for this.

But first, there is one thing I need to do: overcome my fear of Janice. I realize it sounds lame to someone sitting on the outside looking in, but imagine spending the rest of your life knowing that you let someone bully you, humiliate you, make you feel as big as a freckle on a flea's ass, and you did nothing to stop her.

And I'm not talking about the occasional snide comment thrown my way. I'm talking having my panties stolen from my gym locker and hung on the flagpole while I swam laps, enduring a seven-day Tweet attack by "Jgirl," who insisted I was once a boy, and food being thrown at me every day.

I was sick and tired of being the reigning Queen Loser of Los Pinos High, located in the glorious Bay Area burbs of sunny California, for four years in a row. And no way, no how was I about to end high school holding that title.

From this day forward, I would stand up for myself. I would conquer my fears. I would face Janice.

Hey. And who knew? Maybe even Dax, the yummiest guy in school, would notice me. A smile, eye contact, whatever. After pining from afar for four long years, nothing would make me happier or erase my self-imposed Queen Loser title faster.

Of course he'll notice you. You've been doing your affirmations, right?

I took one last look in the mirror and smiled. "That's right, Dakota. This is your day. This is your moment." I turned and tripped over my purse on the floor.

CHAPTER TWO

Mandy waited in her usual spot under the overhang at the front of the school. Her big brown eyes lit up like disco balls when she saw me pull into the lot in my new red car. She immediately ran over to inspect it.

"Ohmygod, it's amazing! And you *look* amazing," she said as I slipped from the car. We hadn't seen each other over spring break because she had gone to Florida to stay with her dad. I ended up at the Hamptons with my aunt, for the third year in a row, due to my dad being away on business and my mother having to work. At least this time I'd whittled the trip down to four days. I told my mom I'd rather be alone at home for my birthday than with her crazy sister.

"Wait. I love the outfit," Mandy critiqued politely. "But I thought you said you got *new* clothes."

"They're new to me."

She rolled her eyes. "If my parents gave me a thousand bucks to spend for my birthday, you wouldn't see me going to a thrift store."

It was true; I had a fetish for retro. Today I wore a 1950s-style pink blazer with three-quarter sleeves and giant pink buttons, along with a vintage Dior rhinestone necklace over a plain tee and jeans.

"I only spent half," I explained. "I thought you could help me attack the mall after school?" I'd really only spent two hundred; three went to the animal shelter for food and new beds. The rest would go toward clothes for college.

Mandy clapped. "Yippy! That's perfect because I got you a gift certificate for H&M!" She loved clothes, which was why she would be going to Parsons in the fall. I was happy for her, but New York City was really far away.

"I knew there was a reason you were my bestie." She gave me a mock kiss on the cheek and trotted off to class.

"See you at lunch." I grabbed my backpack and smiled. *Check.* First five minutes of school were a success. I hoped the next three hundred and eighty five minutes went just as well.

Everything will be great. The universe likes you. Dax will notice you. You are not afraid of Janice. Everything will be great. The universe likes you. Dax will notice you. You are not afraid of Janice… I wandered down the hallway, weaving between students. My feet approached the homeroom doorway, and I had to shift my focus from cheesy, unrealistic affirmations to panic attacks. As in, not having one. My trademark move involved stuttering and hyperventilating. But I'd promised myself that I wouldn't go there.

Have faith, have faith, have…

My nemesis, Janice, was in my homeroom and had been every single, goddamned year. On a good day, she'd show up late and take a seat toward the front, leaving me alone. On a bad day, she'd arrive on time, sit next to me, and peck the feathers from my head. She was truly an evil, sadistic witch. With a *b*. Capitalized. Embossed on a hanky. With snot.

I stopped in the doorway and looked around, relieved beyond belief not to see Janice yet. I needed a few extra moments to call upon my Jedi bitch-repelling skills. There were several other faces I recognized, though. Greg, the tall swimmer guy. Karen, the all-around nice girl who seemed involved in every after-school activity possible—yearbook, fund-raising, dance committee, etc.—and a few other people who had no idea I existed, but didn't pick on me either.

I slid into a seat toward the back and began biting my nails.

Mr. McGregor, my homeroom teacher, walked in, a vision of chaos: hair uncombed, khakis wrinkled, glasses slipping down his nose. He was my fave. He headed up the poetry club and theater. "Dakota," he would always say, "I know high school can be rough, but trust me, things become infinitely better once you get out into the real world. Look at me—I'm happy and successful."

I get that most people would say, "A high school English teacher? Successful? Eh-hem. Sure." But he did what he loved, and it showed. So, yeah, he was successful. At least in my eyes.

"All right, everyone," Mr. M addressed the class. "Welcome back from spring break—"

"Hey, y'all! Wassup?"

Jesus, no.

"Ms. Jensen, so nice of you to join us," said Mr. M.

My heart and central nervous system protested violently at the sight of her. My hands began to sweat and tremble. The air in my lungs felt instantly polluted.

Maybe confronting Janice could wait for another day.

No! You have to do this, I told myself. *You are officially a grown-up, and grown-ups don't back down from bullies.*

But as she took a seat toward the middle of the room, she flung her silky blond locks over her shoulder and flashed a wicked little smile my way. Whoever said an image is worth a thousand words was so right; that image just told me she wanted to make my life hell today. *Show no fear, show no fear, you are Yoda…*

Then a tiny ray of sunlight burst through the dark, wet storm clouds hovering overhead.

*Dax…*I sighed as my mind took yummy-boy roll call. Light brown eyes trimmed with thick brown lashes.

Check.

Sandy-blond, shaggy hair, towel dried and left that way.

Check, check.

Heavenly broad shoulders, well-defined everything—arms, chest, legs—encased in low-slung faded jeans, and a snug tee?

Mmmm…Check.

My mind hit a speed bump and popped out of my little drool fest when I realized the only open seat was right behind me, and Dax was headed straight for it.

I straightened my spine and pasted on a smile as he walked by, smelling sweet and delicious and…

Nutty? I didn't know Snickers made cologne. It totally worked for him.

While I inhaled deeply—guess I was kinda hungry—Dax took his seat, but no notice of me.

That's okay, Dakota. It's going to happen. It's going to happen…

"Hey, Dakota," I heard a voice whisper from behind.

I froze. Had I imagined it?

"Dakota?" he said again.

Yes. Not only had he spoken to me, but he also knew my name. *Yes! Yes! Yes!*

I slowly turned my head over my shoulder and tried not to tremble. Or drool. Or say something dorky. "What's up?" *Nailed it!*

His brown eyes were even more magnificent up close.

"Do you have a pen? I forgot mine," he whispered.

Pen. He wants a pen.

"Sure." I pulled one from the front pocket of my backpack and handed it over. And then it happened. He smiled at me. Actually smiled. Even his little dimples made an appearance.

Freeze image in brain. Die happy now. I felt no shame—zero—admitting that I took this as an omen from the universe. Change was indeed comin' round that mountain. My life was on its way to perfection.

I smiled back and turned toward the front of the class, knowing that I looked like a giant grinning moron, but I didn't care. Dax Price had smiled at me and knew my name.

Still remaining on my high school bucket list was to face that horrible, evil cheer-cow the next time she messed with me. I didn't know when it was coming, but it was coming.

ॐॐ

"Do you like this one?" Mandy looked at the price tag and then held up a satin purple top with ribbons on the back. Her brown eyes twinkled with mischief. Or was that the smugness of victory? I was finally at the mall, letting her pick out clothes for me. A first.

"I'll try it on." Normally I didn't wear purple—sorta looked weird with my red hair—but I was in a super great mood. After homeroom, Janice had taken off, and I didn't see her the entire day.

"So, how was your dad's?" I asked, shuffling through the black skirts a few racks away. I didn't get how Mandy could become so excited about shopping in such a large, well-organized department store. Where was the victory in that? Going to a thrift store or even one of those small, funky boutiques was way more fun, like going on a treasure hunt.

"Okay." She shrugged. "Like usual, he spent most of his time at work. I read. That was about it."

"At least you got to see him every night. That's good, right?"

"I guess," she replied, with stark disappointment. But in all honesty, Mandy had it way better than I did. I was lucky to see my father once a year, although we did Skype a couple times a month. His photography and modeling agency kept him traveling constantly, hopping from one exotic location to the next and then back again to his main office in the UK, where he was originally from. He had his business before marrying my mother, an ER nurse. Ironically, they met while he was in San Francisco on a shoot after he really got shot. Wrong place at the wrong time, except that he ended up in the hospital and met my mother. I liked to think it was fate.

Not so fate-tastic was that every year since I could remember, he threatened to quit the on-location assignments or sell the company to his right hand man. But every year, he kept going. "We need the money," he'd say. Or, "We'll never be able to send you to college and retire." After the age of twelve, I began to understand that he kept working because he wanted to. It wasn't that he didn't love me, but he loved his job more. When I became older, however, I felt sort of thankful he wasn't around so much. Simply put, I loved him, but there were things about him that seriously pissed me off. Things I didn't want to think about.

And how my mother got by? Who knows? I guess she was too busy to feel lonely since she spent her days at the hospital. And being a nurse meant she rarely made it home at a reasonable hour, which is why I spent more time than I should've with a nanny or at Mandy's house while growing up.

"So how about *your* spring break?" Mandy asked, trying to brush her dark hair out of her eyes while balancing a giant heap of clothes on her left arm.

"Other than listening to Aunt Rhonda lecture me ten times a day about the value of youth and how I'm spoiling it by buying into the media's narrow perception of beauty and that she'd give anything to have my ass, rack, and skin? Oh! And being set up with her friends' snobby sons who wanted nothing to do with me?" I shrugged. "I guess it was fine."

"Oh, I bet you just loved that," she said, referring to the fact that my aunt lived in the Hamptons and was obsessed with having a very social lifestyle. I didn't necessarily look down on her, but I didn't understand the need to live my life on the front of a tabloid. I wanted to have a career, travel, fall in love, live a quiet, happy life surrounded by people I loved.

"I went jogging on the beach every morning. That was nice," I finally replied.

She laughed. "Yeah, I bet."

"Well, next year, no Aunt Rhonda's. My father promised to take me to Tokyo."

Did I believe he'd actually take me this time? Maybe not, but it was time to start having faith that change was coming.

Mandy gave me a look as if she knew what I was thinking. "All right, let's try these on." She held out a pile of multicolored blouses and skirts.

I cringed.

"You promised," she warned.

9

That I had. And I'd been stupid enough—likely still suffering from hormonal-bliss overload due to Dax—not to have given Mandy any boundaries like "thou shall not dress me in anything resembling rainbow barf."

I took a deep breath. "I'm trusting you not to make me look like a clown."

"Dakota, seriously? Would I ever do that to you? Besides, have you looked in the mirror lately? You've officially blossomed since Christmas. I could dress you in an orange muumuu and you'd look hot."

Or like a pumpkin gone wrong. And I wouldn't call finally getting boobs and growing an inch—making me a whopping five-five—at the age of eighteen "blossoming." More like catching up. In any case, I appreciated the pep talk.

"Let's get this over with. And stop kissing my ass!" I said.

She squealed with delight. "I've always wanted to dress you. This is going to be so much fun!"

I didn't know about that, but at least this would make Mandy happy. That was something.

CHAPTER THREE

Tuesday.

The next morning, I arrived at school a little later than usual due to a recent alarm clock mishap (I'd "accidentally" shoved it off the nightstand and killed the contraption a few weeks ago. Poor thing.) But I digress. The real reason I'd overslept was that my mother had come home around midnight so I'd gotten up to eat a bowl of cereal and show her my new clothes. What always amazed me about her was that no matter how long her day was, she always had energy to talk and smile. Loved her. And she always looked amazing: her blond hair pulled back neatly into a bun, her face flawless and fresh—no makeup—and her blue eyes bright and alive, just like mine. Minus the bright and alive part.

"The secret, my dear, is being happy. Happiness keeps you young," she always said.

That's why when I saw Janice's face light up with evil intent as I walked into homeroom that morning, and found the last seat was situated right between her and Dax, well, I didn't let it get to me. Janice would be the ugliest troll on the planet by the time b-day number twenty hit; there was clearly no happiness in her life. Too bad for her because I was…

Happy, happy, happy. And ready to stand up for myself.

"Hey, Dakota. Nice skirt," she said nice and loud for everyone to hear. "Salvation Army's finest?" She snickered along with a few other Janice fans in the room.

Actually, it was Neiman's finest, but I wasn't about to let her belittle my love of thrift. *Right Macklemore?*

I looked at her and stared with defiance.

Her big blue eyes were caked with way too much mascara—how the heck did she manage to blink?—and she had her blond hair pulled into a high ponytail. I wanted to rip it out.

Wow, this glaring back feels good! I was just warming up.

"You know it," I finally replied. "In fact, it was hanging right next to that skanky nightmare of a skirt your grandmother donated. She said she never wore it because you bought it for her; she's not into slutty, apparently. But who am I to judge? Especially when the look works so well for you."

Okay. My comeback was wordy. Maybe a little lame, too. But it was the best I could do on the fly, given that being mean wasn't in my box of tricks.

Janice's face turned a pissy shade of red. She hadn't been expecting me to fight back since I never had. Not once in almost four years.

Her eye twitched. "You're pathe—"

"Janice," Dax cut her off, "don't you have a hangnail to file or tiny animal to torture?"

"I…I…" Janice opted for shooting hateful thoughts in his general direction. I'm guessing that was because her shock was as big as mine. Dax had defended me. Me!

I flashed a "thank you smile" his way. He gave me a quick nod and turned his attention toward his book.

As for me? I gloated. Not because Dax had given Janice's ego a big "fuck you," but because I'd been left to fend for myself all these years with no one but Mandy—who was rarely around for the attacks—on my side. Having someone get my back felt…frigging wonderful. Add Dax to that equation and frigging wonderful turned into frigging awesome.

My victory buzz was short-lived, however, because Mr. M gave us our assignment: a writing exercise. "You will write about three things you did this spring break and then read it to the class."

A communal groan erupted.

"This should be easy for you, Dakota," Janice said. "Since you just hung out with a bunch of dirty dogs. Was it fun picking up shit? How do you get it out from under your nails—oh! Wait. That's what that smell is…"

I heard a few small "ewws" from the drama junkies listening in.

That's when it happened. I snapped.

Now, don't get me wrong. Everyone gets mad, especially when they've been picked on as relentlessly as I had, but this was different compared to all those other times Janice had belittled the things I loved. This time she was trying to steal more than my pride; she was trying to steal my hope. I'd really had it.

Rage filled my mind along with images of ripping out her hair. Yes, I would jump on her head and pluck out her golden feathers! *Let's see how she likes it!*

But that's not what happened.

What I chose to do instead would be far worse. The biggest mistake of my life. I lied. Yes. Lied. A big, hairy, Whopper with cheese of a lie. It was one of those moments that as the words poured from my mouth, I caught myself thinking, *Why the hell am I saying this? Not even I would believe such a festering pile of crap!* But once I started, I could not stop.

Why? Why? Why?

My lie would become my life, my prison, my punishment for everything I'd ever done wrong.

CHAPTER FOUR

"You?" Janice laughed. "You have a boyfriend? And you spent spring break with him, going to parties in the Hamptons?" she laughed so hard that tears popped from her eyes like fleas jumping off a dog in a bathtub. "Oh! Oh! That's frigging hysterical."

"Ms. Jensen, care to share what's so funny?" Mr. M peered over the top of his glasses, giving her an annoyed look.

"Yes!" She chuckled. "Dakota says that—wait." She looked at me. "Why don't you tell everyone what you did during break?"

I slouched in my chair and tried to ignore Dax rolling his eyes as if I were the lamest creature on the planet. The rest of the class simply stared with the sort of interest one might have when passing by a car accident.

"Ms. Jensen," Mr. M said, "I'll see you in detention." He made a little circular motion with his hand, indicating she should turn herself around and get to work.

"What?" Janice barked. "Bu...bu...but I have practice after school."

Mr. M shrugged. "Correction. You *had* practice. Would you like to miss tomorrow as well?"

Dax chuckled under his breath, and Janice shot him a nasty look before turning her toxic gaze to me. "Let's get to writing, shall we, Dakota?"

Crap. What would I do now? I had to write an essay about what I'd done over break, and if I didn't retell the outrageous lie I'd just told, then Janice would have a field day. On the other hand, if I did write those lies and read them to the class, everyone would know I'd made them up. It was completely implausible for me to have a boyfriend.

Ugh. Where had those lies come from? What had possessed me to make up that garbage? I mean…really! *Idiot. You're an idiot, Dakota.*

Doing everything in my power not to look at Dax or anyone else, I got up and left.

☜☞

After driving around for an hour and ignoring ten text messages from Mandy, asking what had happened, I finally landed at Starbucks in the next burb over. I couldn't stand to face anyone I knew. *What a moron!* Wait. No. That was too good for me. Freak of nature. Yes, that fit. Again, I couldn't understand what had come over me. I'd been possessed by the demon of obnoxious lies.

Now what would I do? Deny I'd said those things? After, like, ten people overheard me? I pulled out my notebook with the handmade leather jacket—the one my dad had sent me on my sixteenth birthday—and scribbled way. Sometimes writing down my thoughts helped me sort things out.

Options:

Jump off bridge? No. Not my style.

Run away to an exotic island? No passport.

Witness protection program? Ugh. Would have to find a horrible crime to witness—not so easy.

I sighed. Maybe my parents would let me change schools? That would work, right? Except that the other schools in the district were still in Janice territory since she and her cheer-demons belonged to the same cheer-demon club and practiced together. And there was no way my parents would let me change with only eight weeks to go.

Maybe it would all blow over and be forgotten tomorrow?

My phone buzzed again. Another text from Mandy.

Why didn't you tell me you had a boyfriend who's a model? And you're training for the Olympics? I heard you broke the world record running to ur car!

Oh Lord. Now the lie had wings! And a tail! By morning, it would have antennae and, perhaps, a pair of snappy shoes!

Christ almighty. Haven't I suffered enough? I thought, looking up at the industrial-style ceiling and trying to hold back tears.

Okay. Think this through. I'd said that everything happened in the Hamptons. That was way on the other side of the country, so it's not like anyone could check the facts or anything. Maybe after a few days it would all die down.

My phone buzzed again, and I read the message. *Dang it! No!*

According to Mandy, who followed Janice's "twitting," Janice had posted a pic of me.

Oh no! What now? The picture loaded, and there wasn't a gasp loud enough to capture my anguish. Her note said, and I quote, "Dakota's new man and her Hampton friends."

The picture was of a pack of grungy hyenas tearing at a piece of meat.

Why couldn't she leave me alone? Why did she hate me so much? I swear, there was something wrong with that girl. It simply wasn't natural to loathe someone as much as she loathed me for no goddamned reason.

Then I had an idea. A terrible idea. I scribbled it down and stared at the words, letting them infuse my mind while the world zoomed by in fast motion.

Don't do it, Dakota. Don't do it, said that little voice inside my head.

But I wasn't listening.

Head spinning and heart pounding, I took a long sip of my mochaccino and then pulled my laptop from my backpack. What I did next is something I'm not proud of, and I won't ever try to justify it, because there is no justification. I knew, even as I did it, regret would follow. Someday. But sometimes, you just reach your limit and stoop to a level you didn't know existed inside you. You take a bad situation and make it worse. You give in to the *other* voice inside your head that tells you just this once, just this once you have to be bad in order to prove a point.

I am going to hell for this.

But I wasn't hurting anyone, so would I really? I wasn't stealing, or cheating on a test. I was simply going to lie about having a really, really hot boyfriend. One that would make Janice and her friends feel like they were dating my leftovers.

I frantically searched for the picture of the most gorgeous guy I could find. *Bingo!*

I sucked in a breath of worship and studied every masculine inch. Tall, perfect abs, sculpted chest, smooth olive skin, dark eyes, and slightly unkempt black hair falling about his face just so. He was the embodiment of my dream man: seductive, strong, confident, and mysterious. There was something about him that had me instantly fantasizing—who was he? Where was he from? What did his voice sound like?

And his eyes. There was an angry look about them.

Haunted. He's haunted by something.

Ugh. You're an idiot. He's a model. He's probably thinking about a sandwich. Or doing sit-ups.

Well, now he's thinking about you. I saved the picture to my hard drive, created the new profile, and uploaded the image to Facebook.

CHAPTER FIVE

Wednesday.

The next morning, I rolled over in bed and groaned at the window. It was overcast, which always put me in a gloomy mood. It also made me want to stay in my bed where I felt safe and warm.

I lay there half-awake, half in a dream, staring blankly at my whitewashed antique desk in the corner, from which the blank screen of my laptop stared back, beckoning me to charge it.

Laptop!

I sprang from the bed. "No! Please, please, please tell me I didn't do it!" That regret I'd been expecting came a little sooner than I'd hoped.

I fished my phone from my purse on the floor and tapped the app with the big *F*. As the little spinning doughnut danced on my screen, I made a small prayer to the gods of stupidity and asked for forgiveness.

I tapped my Friends page and waited for it to load.

Oh no. Eight. Yesterday, I'd had seven friends—Mandy and a few other random people who I wouldn't exactly call friends. More like people with common interests in saving dogs at kill shelters. But today there was one new name.

The bottom of my world fell out. *Oh no. I did it.*

Santiago Asturias II from Barcelona, Spain, officially tagged as "boyfriend."

Had my mochaccino been roofied? What in the world made me think I could pull a gorgeous photo off the Internet and pass him off as my boyfriend?

I hit my forehead. "Hell is too good a place for me." Couldn't I have at least picked an ugly guy? Oh, but noooo. I picked the hottest man ever to exist. Yes! A man! And no way was he close to my age!

All would not have been so lost if I'd not also made my profile public and connected it to Twitter right before I posted @Jgirl *Bite me, Janice Jensen.*

I knew she'd see it. I knew she'd want to retaliate. I knew she'd go to my Facebook page and check out my friends.

I covered my face. *Why, why, why did I get myself into this mess?* Because, hand-on-Bible truth? This was so not me. Not. Me. I'd never been the sort of person to lie my way through an issue. Once, when I was seven, I took a sneak peek inside the big red box under the Christmas tree. It was a new dollhouse. When my mother asked me who'd opened the present, I lied. I'd felt so guilty that I wrote Santa a letter stating—one hundred times—that I would never lie again. Never lie again, never lie again, never…

Sorry, Santa, I guess I broke that *promise.*

My cell vibrated. Another text from Mandy. *Where r u?*

I sighed. *Dying on the inside.*

What happened?

Janice, I replied.

She's saying terrible things about you.

"Welcome her to the club," I said as tweets rolled in. Apparently five other egg-faced people I'd never met were also saying "terrible things." *How odd.*

I deserve it, I responded.

So, no supermodel boyfriend? she asked.

No.

Too bad. He's way hot.

U saw him?

Everyone saw him. Janice tweets and Instagrams like a pro.

What do I do? I asked, once again feeling eternally grateful for Mandy's friendship. Notice how she hadn't judged me. And given her intelligence, she'd probably deduced the reason behind my ridiculous yet uncharacteristic behavior.

Several minutes passed without a reply, and then...

People will forget. Eventually.

Eventually? Eventually? Pfff... Not likely. This stupid move would follow me to the grave. This was not how I'd envisioned beginning the journey into adulthood!

I tapped my finger on the side of the phone. I had no choice but to face "people" and not let it break me. For sure, though, I'd learned one valuable lesson: I would never lie again. I was better than this.

I threw on a sweatshirt and jeans before trudging off to the bathroom. I wrangled my red curly mop into a sloppy ponytail, brushed my teeth, and glared at the girl staring back.

Loser.

I took off my clothes and crawled back into bed. If I couldn't face myself, how could I face anyone else?

࿔

Thursday.

"Times up, Dakota!"

My mother pulled down the blanket and rolled me off the bed onto the floor with a thump.

"Ow!" I tried to return to my sanctuary of sadness, but she grabbed me by the earlobe and yanked me up.

"I know you're not sick. You are going to school today, young lady."

I tried to twist away, but the woman had a grip of iron. "I'm not going."

She shuffled me toward my private bathroom. "I don't know what's going on, but you're not spending the rest of your life in bed, hiding out. I didn't raise a coward."

She may not have raised me like that, but I'd ended up a coward anyway.

I looked at her out of the corner of my eye. "I screwed up."

She let go. "Christ, Dakota. You're pregnant? Why didn't you tell me?" She lowered her head and covered her face with both hands. "I should've guessed."

"What? No! Oh my God."

Her eyes opened up like giant balloons. "Drugs! Damn it, Dakota! Haven't you heard enough horror stories from me? And you're eighteen now. Do you have any idea what'll happen if they catch you? "

"No, Mom, I'm not pregnant. I'm not on drugs. Although, I'd really love a very strong tranquilizer…for you!"

Spite flickered in her eyes. "Then what? Why are you acting like this?"

I sighed. "I lied and everyone knows it."

She stared at me. "Lied. To a teacher? Your principal?"

I shook my head. "I wish." I let out a long breath and sat on the bed. "I told everyone I am seeing this guy, but I'm not."

She laughed.

"What?" I spat. Was it so hard to believe, even for my own mother?

"I'm relieved."

"Nice," I said.

"Think of it from my standpoint. You've been a model daughter. Good grades. No rebelling. Responsible. I kept wondering when my luck would run out. And now, you're saying you lied to a few friends about a boy?"

"Mom! This is serious!"

"Right. You're telling an ER nurse who watches mothers lose their kids to drunk drivers or drug ODs that this little issue is serious?"

Okay. When she put it like that…

"Maybe I am being petty," I admitted. "But you have no idea what I've been through. Those girls are complete, fucking bitches."

"Dakota! Watch that tongue."

"What? Like you don't use those words?"

She smiled. "Of course I do. I'm a nurse. But I'd never use them with my mother. If she were alive."

Touché. "Sorry."

"Listen, baby. Whatever you did, you can't run forever. Just treat it like a Band-Aid and rip that thing off. If that doesn't go well, focus on the fact that it's the end of the school year. You'll be off to San Diego in the fall, studying pre-law, and high school will be nothing but a distant memory."

As usual, she was right; my dream of going away to college was just around the corner, and I couldn't wait. It had been my mental sanctuary for years, the Promised Land where I could be geeky and academic and finally start living my life. This immature high school world of drama and popularity contests would evaporate the moment the principal slapped that diploma in my hand. Bottom line, none of this stuff really mattered, except for the grades. That didn't mean, however, that these final weeks weren't going to suck monkey balls.

"Bring me a few gallons of ice cream tonight?" I asked.

She hugged me. "Sure. Now get your ass to school."

☙❧

When I pulled into the entrance of the parking lot, it was drizzling and four minutes to the bell.

"What? Come. On!" It looked like two jocks were fighting over something—*the size of their tiny straps?*—and the cars had stopped to watch, creating a giant logjam. Oh well. Not like I was in a hurry to face Janice.

I glanced toward the school's overhang, relieved to see Mandy in her usual spot. She made a sympathetic little wave as if trying to assure me all would be okay. Earlier, I'd shot her a text, letting her know I was returning to hell school, ready to face the fiery inferno of my sins. She'd replied with a simple happy face, and now it was her real happy face providing me the fortitude I needed.

My heart raced, knowing that today would be the most humiliating day of my life, and there was no getting around it. Served me right. I'd stooped to Janice's level, and now I'd pay the price.

"Finally," I hissed. The cars moved, and I slipped into the first available spot toward the back of the lot. I turned off the engine and grabbed my bag, not bothering to check my hair or makeup. What was the point?

I locked the car and started the death march through the lot toward my fate. With each step, that witness protection program sounded better and better. Couldn't be *that* hard to get in on a federal crime and turn informant, could it? Perhaps I would Google "snitch" on my lunch break if I wasn't too busy dodging apple cores from the masses.

"Dakota! Watch out!" I heard Mandy yell, but by the time my brain caught up with my eyes, it was too late.

I screamed, but it wasn't because a large blue pickup barreled down on me; it was because of whom I saw standing next to my best friend.

Smack!

"Dakota? Dakota? Ohmygod. Are you okay?" Mandy's face was a pale blur against the backdrop of the gray rain clouds overhead. I felt the wind dust my face, chilling the drizzle collecting on my cheeks. "Don't move. Okay? The ambulance will be here in a minute."

Luckily, the hospital was exactly one block from school; however, a paramedic wasn't what I needed. A psychiatrist was more like it.

Although I couldn't make out the face clearly, the image hovering directly to my right looked eerily familiar.

"Santiago?" I mumbled.

I will never, ever forget the sound of his voice. Deep, strong, one hundred percent male.

Mesmerizing.

Something embedded in its timbre called out to millions of years of female evolution. It penetrated so deeply that even in my state of utter delirium, I could've sworn he'd latched onto my soul and wrapped it around his pinky.

"Dakota," he responded, with a thick Spanish accent, "don't move. Everything will be all right."

That was the last thing I remember before I blacked out.

CHAPTER SIX

"Honey, can you hear me? Dakota? Open your eyes, baby." A warm hand ran down the length of my arm.

My vision focused slowly, but my mother's calm face punched through the haze. Was this what people witnessed when they came into the ER, or even died? My mother's loving expression, reassuring them that they would be all right?

"What happened?" I whispered.

"You were in an accident, but everything's fine—just a concussion. How do you feel?"

I made a pathetic little nod and tried to focus my eyes on the objects around the room: a small television mounted to the wall behind my mother and a peach-colored table and chair in the corner next to the empty bed at my side. "My head hurts, but fine."

"Good!" She pinched my arm so hard that I yelped. Bolts of fury exploded from her eyes. "What the *hell* were you *thinking*?" She pinched me again.

"Ow!" I sincerely hoped this wasn't her usual bedside manner. Not only did it totally suck, but in no way did it inspire me to stay alive. Although, maybe I did want to get away, so that was something.

I slowly sat up and then rubbed my head. *Owww…* "It was an accident. You just said so."

My mother covered her face. "I knew this would happen. Damn it. He promised."

"What? Who promised what?" I groaned, massaging my temples.

She shook her head from side to side and whisked away the tears from under her eyes. "Nothing. I just wish your father were here. I'm mad. That's all. Never mind." She pasted on a plastic smile.

Okay. That response seemed slightly...*off.* "Mom. I'm sorry. I don't know what happened."

Once again, her eyes filled with an undercurrent of anger. "Well I do. And it won't ever happen again."

"I'm not planning on letting it." My brain completely hurt, and my body was in no better shape.

Just then, Mandy burst into the room. "Jesus Christ Superstar, Dakota. Are you okay?"

I tried not to laugh because (a) it was inappropriate and (b) it would hurt. But it was near impossible to ignore one of Mandy's trademark expressions. She had serious flair for all things Broadway. New York really did seem like the best place for her to go to school.

My mother stood and smoothed down the front of her blue scrubs, too distracted to notice that Mandy had entered the room. "I'll be back to check on you in an hour."

"Okay." As soon as she left, I stopped hiding my panic. I looked at Mandy. "What the hell happened? And why is my mom acting so weird?"

Mandy rolled her eyes and plunked down on the edge of the bed. "You were hit by a car. What did you expect? A polka dance?"

I survived, didn't I? "No, but—"

And then that's when I remembered.

Santiago.

Lord. How had I forgotten?

"Mandy?" I gripped her hand for dear mental life. "Who was standing next to you when I got hit?"

Mandy made a little laugh. "Wow. Janice really *did* hit you hard."

"Janice? Janice hit me?" I asked.

"Um, yeah. Didn't anyone tell you?"

"Obviously not," I replied.

Mandy's dark brown eyes lit with joy. "Janice is in juvie."

"What?"

"She ran you over, Dakota. Everyone saw it. And the only reason she's not in jail is because she's not eighteen yet. Lucky bitch. But according to the rumor mill, she's supposed to be on meds and stopped taking them. Bipolar or something like that."

"So she tried to kill me?" I knew she hated me, but murder? Really?

Mandy nodded. "Supposedly, she'd told all her friends she wanted to 'kill you' for making her look stupid in front of Dax."

Okay. I knew it sounded strange for me to defend Janice, but I couldn't believe she wanted to kill me. Meds or no meds. Not for something like that. "I'm sure she meant it figuratively." Pause. Think. Rethink. "Are you sure?"

Mandy nodded.

Christ. I can't believe it!

"Santiago and I saw the whole thing," she added. "By the way, why did you lie to me?"

Santiago? "Wha…what…what?"

"Yeah. He went to the station to make a statement, but I'm sure he'll be here any minute."

"Whoa! Back up. Who's at the station?"

Her brows lifted. "Saantiaagooo," she said with exaggerated slowness, as if speaking to a brand-new foreign exchange student. "You *really* must've hit your head hard if you can't remember your secret, hot boyfriend. Personally, I can't stop thinking about him. I sooo want one! I mean, seriously, does he have a brother? Even a younger one? 'Cause I can wait! If Jacob can do it for Renesmee, so can I!"

What the… "Huh?"

"Hey! Don't judge me. I never knew that actual human beings could be that good-looking." Mandy huffed. "So. Not. Fair. By the way, exactly why were you hiding him from me?"

I plopped back against the headboard—*ow!*—in complete shock.

"You okay, Dakota? Should I call your mom?"

I shook my head. "No. I'm…I'm just tired."

Mandy covered my hand and smiled. "You should rest before Santiago gets here. Wouldn't want him seeing you looking all squiggly faced like that." She leaned in and kissed my cheek. "I'll stop by before school tomorrow."

Before I could say another word, she was gone, leaving me with the insane thoughts plowing through my mind.

Boyfriend? Janice is in jail for attempted murder?

The only explanation was that I was in a coma and this was all a dream. *But you saw Santiago before the car hit you. Was that a dream, too?*

My phone vibrated on the beige Formica nightstand. I picked it up and stared at the caller ID.

Santiago.

My hand trembled so fiercely that I could barely hold the darn thing to my ear. "Y…y…yes?"

"Hey, baby. Miss me?"

"Who is this?" I whispered.

Long pause. "*Tsk. Tsk.* Have you forgotten me so soon? Check your Facebook page," he said, his voice deep, menacing.

My heart slammed into overdrive, but I couldn't seem to make my mouth move.

"No worries," he said. "I'll be there in five to refresh your memory."

The call ended, but all I could do was stare at the phone.

This can't be happening.

CHAPTER SEVEN

Lord. Whoever had been on the other end of that phone was coming to my room. I had to get out of there. Because as much as I loved believing in miracles, those didn't exist, which meant this guy was some psychopathic stalker, some frigging lunatic who'd convinced everyone he was my boyfriend.

I slipped from the covers and immediately had to brace myself on the edge of the hospital bed. My head pulsed with painful, dizzying jabs. I slowly stood upright and willed myself steady. My ribs and hip were sore, but I'd survive. That was, if I got the heck out there.

I blew out a breath and wobbled to the clear plastic bag with my belongings, hanging on the wall. I had to find my mother. I had to warn her. What if this guy showed up and tried something?

I slipped on my jeans, sweatshirt, and sneakers, not bothering with the other stuff. I grabbed my phone and purse and tiptoed to the door.

I poked my head out, hoping to spot my mother doing rounds, but instead I saw—

The breath whooshed from my lungs. *Santiago?*

Cue slow motion and avalanche of conflicting, irrational thoughts accompanied by an imminent panic attack.

My stomach and heart squeezed into a brick and then dropped through the center of my body.

Lord, help me.

Because the man I'd invented—correction—the *gorgeous* man I'd stolen a picture of, stood twenty feet away, speaking to my mother, wearing low-slung faded jeans and a fitted white, button-down shirt.

I stared in wonderment while my eyes infused with his image and branded itself on my brain. He was lust, rock star, tough guy, jock, Prince Charming, and misfit rolled into one dangerous, rugged, well-groomed package. He sent my female brain into a tailspin.

I've lost my mind. That gorgeous man is not standing there. That's not possible!

I willed my heavy feet to move, but my eyes remained glued to him. He was tall—around six three or six four—and, just like in his photo, built like a lean, mean predatory animal with broad shoulders and powerful-looking…everything. Especially those arms. And those legs. And those…*yep. Everything*. To boot, he stood with the sort of confidence that gave me the distinct impression he really might be deadly. And ate his meat raw. Possibly still squealing.

Santiago, who towered over my mother, leaned down and hugged her. Then my mother said something, and they laughed like old friends.

What? He hugged my mother? What was happening? Did she know him? Was the universe punishing me for lying? If it was, it was totally working. I'd never, ever lie again. *This time, I mean it, Santa.*

Okay. This was all just too weird. I needed to get the heck out of there to rearrange my head. I slipped into the hallway, walking briskly in the opposite direction of Santiago.

Exit! I flew into the stairwell and made my way outside. The afternoon air felt warm and soothing on my skin. I took in a slow breath to calm my pounding head, but it had the opposite effect. What a wallop I must've had.

Okay. Try to think. Where would I go, and how would I get there? I didn't have my sanity. I didn't have a clue. I didn't have much money.

I looked inside my purse. *But I still have my keys and a full tank of gas.* The school was one block away, as was my car.

Head throbbing and body aching, I half jogged, half hobbled the short distance to my salvation. Everyone was in class, so despite the parking lot being full of vehicles, it had an eerie feel, amplifying my state of panic.

No. Keep calm. This isn't real. This isn't real. This isn't—

My phone buzzed in my pocket, causing me to jump. I looked at the screen. *Shit. Santiago.*

No. No. I wasn't going to answer. My brain knew none of this was real. I only needed to go somewhere and think, calm myself so I'd wake up.

I got to my car and slipped inside. I fumbled with the keys as my hand trembled uncontrollably.

"Where the *hell* do you think you're going? Have you lost your fucking mind?" he said, jumping into the passenger seat.

I couldn't speak. I couldn't move. And I'm pretty sure my mouth hung open.

Santiago stared with those dark eyes surrounded by thick black lashes—the exact ones I remember picking out from some random Internet page and saving to my hard drive. I didn't know the man, but I knew he was unhappy by the way his broad chest heaved and his nostrils flared like a bull about to gore a matador.

"I…I…" The words weren't forming. I wanted them to, but my throbbing brain and sweating, trembling body simply couldn't reconcile the torrential rain of emotions pouring into me.

He reached over and plucked the keys from the ignition. "You've been in an accident. Why did you leave the hospital? And what makes you think you should be getting behind the wheel of a fucking car?"

"I…I…" I still couldn't speak.

He shook his head and mumbled under his breath. He got out of the car, walked over to my side, and opened the door. "Out."

But I couldn't let go of the steering wheel. It felt real and familiar. If I let go, I might start screaming. For Christ's sake, the man even smelled like the delicious concoction of leather and citrus I'd imagined when I'd made him up.

He leaned down and put his hand on my forehead. "Hell, you feel hot, Dakota. Move the fuck over."

He pushed me to the passenger side. Meanwhile, my mind went around and around and around until the space between my ears felt like pea soup. He turned on the ignition, backed out of the spot, and headed to the hospital. His phone immediately buzzed, and he dug it out of his front pocket. "Yes, Mrs. Dane. I found her. We'll be right there."

My mother had his cell number? Yes, this was a dream, I thought, and closed my eyes. *It's a product of the accident and a very bad fever. Delirium. Yes, wonderful, glorious delirium!*

He pulled into a spot at the hospital's entrance, where my mother waited with a wheelchair, frowning. At least that was something familiar to me. Although, when that look appeared on her face, I knew I was in deep trouble. About two years ago, I had snuck out with Mandy to see *The Rocky Horror Picture Show* at midnight in Berkeley. When I came home covered in bread crumbs and soaking wet from Mandy's water pistol, that frown had been there to greet me. Just like now. But why? Did she think I was just goofing off and playing a joke on her or something? Couldn't she see the genuine panic in my eyes?

"Dakota? Can you hear me?" Santiago snapped his fingers.

I looked at him reluctantly, afraid he might seem all too real. But he wasn't real. He wasn't. "Who are you?" I hissed.

His head drooped and his dark hair fell over his eyes. "This is never going to work." He pushed back his hair with one hand and then looked at me; studied me, actually.

"What?" What had he said?

His inquisitive expression soured. "You're a mess, that's what I said."

No, he'd said this would never work. What had he meant?

He broke eye contact, leaned forward, and nodded at my mother, who opened the passenger door.

"Have you lost your mind? Out, young lady," she fumed.

Oh my God. Was everyone in on this? Had *Invasion of the Body Snatchers* been based on real events? Because that's what this felt like.

Crud. Don't panic. I slipped from the car into the wheelchair, but my mother didn't say another word, which meant she was beyond completely furious. Silence was reserved for only the most extreme offenses, like the time I crashed her car into the neighbor's fence because I was late to a fund-raiser for the animal shelter.

Santiago came around. "I'll take her back, Mrs. Dane, and make sure she doesn't leave this time."

My mother nodded and walked off, not bothering to look back at me.

"Mom? Mom? Where are you going?" I called out but she didn't respond, and she disappeared inside.

I looked up at my captor, searching for some explanation, some clue about who had kidnapped my reality. But when my eyes met with his, there was a moment when something flickered in my head. A moment of recognition or a feeling, really, that I knew him from somewhere beyond just the photo. But that couldn't be right. It couldn't be. Perhaps my mind was making up lies as a coping mechanism, trying to sort out the jumbled facts threatening to undo my sanity.

This very bad dream was turning into a very creepy nightmare.

CHAPTER EIGHT

As Santiago wheeled me back to the room, I tried to contain my fear. Although I knew none of this could be real, it sure the heck felt like it was—right down to the busy doctors, nurses, and patients going about their day, taking no notice of little old me. The only thing people seemed to notice was Mr. tall, dark, and scary-as-shit-but-handsome behind me. Every woman within eyeshot tripped over herself or stopped and stared at Santiago who, by the way, acted completely oblivious.

He pushed me into the room and closed the door. "Put the gown back on and get back into bed," he commanded.

I slowly rose from the wheelchair and avoided looking at him. The hair on my arms and on the back of my neck stood straight up, as if my body instinctually knew danger was near.

"Now," he barked and shoved the blue gown over my shoulder.

Did he really expect me to undress in front of him?

"Can you turn around?" I asked, my voice trembling.

There was no reply.

I glanced over my shoulder, terrified to look at the man. Perhaps because he wasn't a man, but a beast in a man's skin. Or a demon only pretending to be human. Whatever he was, it couldn't be the image perceived by my eyes. That image was of a guy, flesh and bone, so beautiful that I wanted to weep at his feet.

Santiago stood watching me with a feral, dark gaze, leaning against the door, arms crossed against his broad chest.

A deep, dark shiver quaked through me. "Who are you?" I whispered.

He shook his head. "I am your boyfriend. Says so right on Facebook. Now, dress."

But I couldn't. I couldn't bring myself to strip off my clothes in front of this terrifying stranger, especially given that I had nothing on under my jeans and sweatshirt.

I stepped over to the bed and slipped in with my clothes still on. I looked up at Santiago—if that was even this guy's name—and waited for whatever he'd do to me.

He smiled in a displeased sort of way. "You're not used to anyone telling you what to do, but you'll learn." He turned and reached for the door. "I'll make sure of that."

"Who are you?" This time, I demanded. Where had the courage to speak to him like that come from?

He stilled and slowly looked at me, his espresso eyes filled with a lethal tinge. "Lesson *numero uno*, Dakota: Don't ask that question again. Ever."

"But I picked your picture off the Internet. Who—"

He gave me a look that indicated he might hurt someone—me—if I said another word. "I'm going to say this one more time, Dakota. Just once." He held up his index finger. "Stop asking questions. This isn't a joke. Unless you consider death a joke. I. Am. Your. Boyfriend."

He left the room, but his menacing vibe stuck to my skin like campfire smoke sticks to your clothes and hair.

Death? Had he just threatened to kill me?

I pulled the covers up under my chin, trying not to break down while I thought through options. I could call the police, but given that everyone believed this guy was my boyfriend, I'd only look like a nut farmer. I could call Mandy and have her take me to her house where I could hide out, but I suspected Santiago would only find me and drag me back. Or I could wait until my mother returned and talk to her. Yes, she'd know what to do. I had to believe I could trust her despite her anger.

The doctor, an older, lanky man with silver hair, entered the room and interrupted my plotting. Santiago stood next to the door, watching me with those penetrating eyes, as if warning me not to make a scene.

"How's the headache?" the doctor asked, flashing his penlight in my right eye.

I nodded quickly. "Fine. Good. It's good. Maybe just a little dizzy." Okay. I was a lot dizzy, but I wanted to get out of there.

The doctor pulled out my chart from a slot at the foot of the bed. "Well, it looks like you had a reaction to the medication we gave you. But your blood pressure is normal and fever is under a hundred and one. You should be released later today."

"What time?" I asked.

"Not sure yet. We need to observe you for a few more hours."

He slipped his penlight into his pocket. "Until then, young lady, you need to get some rest."

"Wait." I wanted to ask if hallucinations were a side effect or if people lost their minds after being hit by a car and telling really stupid lies at school. But the moment the word *wait* left my lips, Santiago's back straightened. His eyes narrowed and drilled into me from across the room, spiking my brain with instant fear.

"Yes?" the doctor asked.

"I...I..." *I'm afraid for my life. Somebody please help me.* "I'm hungry. Can I eat something?"

The doctor gave me a funny look. "I'll ask one of the nurses to bring you lunch."

"Thanks," I eked out.

Santiago quietly watched as the doctor exited the room. "You heard him. Get some rest." He walked over, and I instinctively wanted to run.

"Don't even think about it," he growled.

Could he read my thoughts? Or was he simply reacting to the terror in my eyes?

He pushed the adjuster on the side of the bed until I was completely horizontal. "Rest," he commanded in a deep voice that sent little pinpricks rushing through my body. I actually was sleepy, like I just might die if I didn't close my eyes.

Maybe just for a moment…

After all, the man was not about to let me leave, and I needed to gather my wits.

When I reopened my eyes, it was dark outside. How long had I slept?

I quickly surveyed the room, hoping my jailer might be gone, but no such luck. He sat in a chair next to the door, eyes closed, arms crossed, head resting back against the peach-colored wall.

I studied him carefully, looking for any signs of what or who he truly was.

A ghost?

But he was a solid mass.

A dream?

Nothing indicated I was still asleep. I saw only a man. Real, breathing, beautiful to a fault—thick lashes fanning out from his eyes, dark straight brows, a masculine jaw, and a chin with a tiny dimple. And his size, well, he certainly was no teenager. He looked to be about twenty. Perhaps as old as twenty-two. And with his lean muscular frame, he looked like he worked out. A lot.

Ghosts don't need to work out.

See. That was the part that didn't make sense. I'd made him up. I mean, yes, the photo had to come from somewhere, so the man physically existed in the world. But he was a random stranger I'd never met. So why was he sitting in my room, guarding me, and acting like he just might rip off my head if I so much as breathed the wrong way?

Lord, the more I thought about it, the weirder and scarier the situation felt.

"Good, you're awake."

I jumped and held my hand over my heart.

"Your mother came by earlier. She said you've been released." He rose from the chair and walked over to the hook on the wall that held my purse and the clear bag that contained only my panties and bra. I hoped he didn't notice or look at them.

"She did? Why didn't she wake me up?" I needed to talk to her. I needed to hear that this was all just some horrible joke.

"She wanted you to rest. She asked me to take you home when you woke up."

Home. He was coming home with me? "I want to see her," I stated quietly, trying not to provoke him.

"She's finishing her shift. You'll see her later tonight."

To heck with provoking...Survive. "I'm not going anywhere with you."

He handed me my purse and flashed a wicked little smile. "Why not?"

Why not? Why not? Oh my. Let's make a list. Shall we? You're scary. And imaginary. And you're scary. I said that already. "Because I have no idea who you are."

He leaned over me, placing his cheek next to mine. "Then let me fill you in," he whispered in my ear. "I'm your boyfriend, and you love me. So don't cause any problems, Dakota."

Adrenaline pumped through my muscles, urging me to run. "And if I do?"

He ran his finger along my jaw, his rough stubble scraping against my cheek. "Do you really want to find out?"

My stomach churned and cramped. I'd never been more frightened of anyone or anything in my entire life. "N...n...no."

He released a heavy breath into my ear. "Because if you challenge me, if you keep asking questions, it won't be pretty. I know all your secrets, Dakota," he whispered. "Every one of them. So think hard about which ones you want to get out."

I felt beads of sweat erupt on my forehead. "Wha...what do y...you mean?"

He pulled back a bit, and annoyance flickered in his eyes. "You were sixteen. You took the BART train into San Francisco with Mandy. Do you want me to go on?"

My jaw dropped. No. I didn't. What I saw that day was horrible. We'd ditched class and snuck off to Saks in the city.

As Mandy and I came around the corner, I saw my dad leaving a hotel right there in Union Square with a blond. Not my mother. He kissed her passionately, and then they went in separate directions. Mandy had been too busy staring at a passing cable car to notice, thank goodness. At first, I tried telling myself that whatever happened in my parent's personal life didn't affect me, but that was silly. How could I ever trust him again? My mother worshipped him—waited for months to see him while he galloped the globe on photo shoots. All the while, he cheated on her.

Not only wouldn't I trust *him*, I wouldn't trust any man. After all, if you couldn't trust your own father, then who? Things were never the same again between us. It was almost like he sensed that I'd discovered his secret.

"But how do you know?" I asked Santiago. My father hadn't seen me. I never told anyone. Ever.

"I know everything, Dakota. The question is, do you want your mother to know everything, too?"

Bastard. If my mother found out my dad had cheated on her, it would break her heart.

"No," I replied, gritting my teeth.

"Then who am I?"

I stared into his eyes. I had to find a way out of this. "My boyfriend."

"Good girl." He grabbed my arm and helped me from the bed.

Not knowing what else to do, I nodded cautiously and left with my captor.

CHAPTER NINE

"How can you stand eating that shit?" Santiago stared from across our antique, country-style kitchen table. It was surreal to see such a lethal-looking man sitting in our cozy, homey kitchen. But then again, nothing about this situation fit.

Knowing my body needed food, I forced myself to take a large bite of my microwaved veggie burger and chewed, ignoring his question. How I managed to swallow anything, I didn't know. My stomach had been in huge knots from the moment we'd left the hospital and headed straight for my house. Yes, he knew where I lived, like he'd driven to my sandstone-colored stucco house, which looked like all the others on the block, a thousand times. He'd even pulled into my spot, right of the garage. When we got to the front door, he took out a set of keys from his pocket to open it. The guy had my house key. I immediately headed for my room, hoping I could hole up inside, but he'd grabbed my hand and pulled me toward the kitchen. "You need to eat something," he'd scolded.

And now, he simply stared with disgust, watching me chew, and I couldn't help my stomach from plummeting and clenching or my hands from shaking.

Nervous as hell, I looked up at the clock on the wall. Normally, my mother came home around midnight. It was a quarter to.

I choked down another bite and focused my eyes on the table, avoiding eye contact. Somehow, someway I needed to figure out what I was going to do. What if this guy never left? *Be brave. Be brave. Start asking questions.* "Are you staying tonight?" I blurted out.

"Are you inviting me?" he asked.

I gasped and looked him.

"Didn't think so," he responded dryly. "I plan to stay until your mother gets home. Then I have business to attend to."

He was going to leave? Thank God. And he had business at this hour? Probably had puppies to strangle or a bank to rob.

I heard the front door open and then close. My mother was home. I rushed to greet her and threw my arms around her neck.

"Dakota, why aren't you in bed yet?" She peeled me off her. "You need to be resting."

"Mom, I need to tell you—"

"Eh-hem," Santiago appeared in the foyer behind me.

My mother's face lit up. "Oh, Santiago. Thank you so much for keeping an eye on Dakota."

Why did she trust him? What lies could he have possibly told her that would grant instant access to "the circle of trust" as De Niro would say?

"It was my pleasure." His smile was deceivingly warm and charming. He put his arm around me. "I'm just glad she's all right." He kissed the top of my head, sending tiny shivers down my spine—the bad kind.

"Well, I'll let you two say your good nights, but then off to bed with you." My mother walked upstairs to her room.

Santiago's sweet expression soured, and he backed me into the wall with his large body. "Whatever you're thinking of doing, Dakota," he hissed quietly in my ear, "don't."

But once he was gone, there was nothing he could say that would keep me from telling her what had really happened or from asking her why she thought this guy was my boyfriend.

He gripped my shoulders firmly, and I felt his rough whiskers scrape against my cheek. "I see that playing nice was a mistake, so let me lay out all my cards." His voice lowered an octave, triggering my knees to tremor. "If you tell her you don't know me, *someone's* going to get hurt. And I'm not speaking about your little secret, Dakota."

Okay, I was wrong. There was something he *could* say. He could tell me again that my mother having her heart broken was the least of my worries.

"Dakota? Do. You. Understand?"

I nodded yes.

"Very good. Get some rest. I'll be back to take you to school on Monday."

That was in four days. Oh, thank heavens. By then I could figure out all this, couldn't I? Yes. If he'd just leave, I would calm down and find a solution.

I watched his large frame leave my house, and it took every ounce of strength I had not to collapse right there on the floor and cry.

Four days. Four days, and he would be back.

ॐॐ

After a long, hot shower, my pulse began to slow to an almost normal rhythm, and I felt like I could breathe again. No, I couldn't risk telling my mother anything, but perhaps she could tell me more about what happened after the car hit me. What had Santiago told her? If they'd only just met, why did she believe he was really my boyfriend?

I slipped on my favorite pink nightie—the one with little black puppies—and wrapped a towel on my head. I looked in the mirror. Without a doubt, I'd been hit by a car. I hadn't noticed before, but there was a dark bruise just above my left brow.

I slipped the neck of my gown off my shoulder and inspected the purple and black pear-shaped mark. Janice had really done this to me? I still couldn't believe it. I mean, malicious was one thing, but murderous was in another camp altogether. Perhaps the rumors had been true; she had mental issues and had gone off her meds.

I reached for my doorknob, planning to go find my mother, when my cell phone rang. *Santiago* flashed across the screen. My entire body tensed up as I thought about not answering it. But if I didn't, would he come back to my house? He seemed like the exact kind of person who might do that.

I answered, but didn't say anything.

"How are you feeling?" his voice sounded irritated.

He wanted to know how I felt? "Terrified."

"You remember what I told you, right babe?"

Babe. He called me babe. Like we were sweethearts. I didn't know how to respond, so I didn't.

"Look out your window," he said.

My pulse revved as I walked over and looked down at the sidewalk. The tall, dark shadow of a man leaned against a motorcycle of gleaming chrome under the moonlit sky.

"I won't be far, Dakota." Had he meant that as a threat? Or to comfort me?

I nodded and backed away from the blinds.

"Now get some rest," he commanded.

The call ended, and I sat on the bed. "This isn't happening. He's not real…"

Afterward, I lay there, trying to solve the puzzle, but got nowhere. Eventually, I drifted off and dreamed of another life. I imagined it was the one I might've had if things hadn't taken such a drastic turn. Instead of being hit by a car, I showed up at school and ran into Janice outside of homeroom. She and her friends laughed at me, which I expected, but when I saw Dax's face as I entered the class, that's when it really stung. Maybe it was pity or disdain, but the look in his eyes made me feel hollow. Ashamed.

Maybe my new alternate reality wasn't so bad after all.

CHAPTER TEN

Friday.

"Honey, I'm leaving for work now," my mother's calm and cheery voice infiltrated my deep sleep. "Mandy also left you a note—she stopped by before school, but I didn't want to wake you."

I looked at my nightstand, but there was still no clock so I looked at my phone instead. It was well past noon.

"And," she added, "your father texted this morning. Says he'll FaceTime you as soon as he checks into his hotel in Shanghai. Probably around 10:00 p.m. our time."

He'd been in Australia earlier in the week, so I knew that meant he'd be tired. But he generally Skyped or FaceTimed with me every two weeks. In another month he was due home, so I'd see him.

"Okay. Rest." She kissed my forehead. "I love you, honey."

"Wait. Mom."

She was almost to the doorway. "Uh-huh?"

"It's about Santiago."

She smiled. "He's in the kitchen, making you breakfast."

"He is?"

"He called this morning and said his schedule freed up so he asked to keep you company."

Terrified, I just stared. I didn't know what to say. This was bad. Really, really bad. What if this guy didn't leave? Would I have to run? Give up my life to get away from him? Not that my current life was oh-so-wonderful, but I had plans. College. My new life.

I sighed deeply. How the hell did I get myself into this? Just a few days ago, the most important things in my life were telling off some stupid girl and getting a guy to smile at me. None of that seemed important now. My entire life

44

had taken a trip down the rabbit hole, and I just wanted to dig myself out before it ruined my plans for a future. I deserved the happiness that awaited me. I'd worked damned hard for it.

"Is everything all right?" she asked.

I knew Santiago was in the other room. If I told her the truth—or what I believed to be the truth—would Santiago really tell her about my dad? Would he really hurt me?

Shit. "Nothing. I guess I'm still freaked out," I said.

"That's a very normal reaction. You almost died yesterday," she replied. "But you have nothing to worry about. You're safe. Alive. And that Janice girl is in custody. If she ever comes near you again, there'll be hell to pay."

Wow. I'd never heard my mom say an angry word about anyone.

I bobbed my head. "Can you come home early tonight?" I didn't want to spend any more time than necessary with Santiago.

Her sparkling blue eyes studied me for a moment. "Okay. I'll do my best, but I want you in bed—alone—before I get home."

Alone? Did she seriously think I was sleeping with that scary guy? "Mom, you really don't have to worry about that."

She looked at me as if I had not one, not two, but three heads growing from my neck.

"What?" I asked defensively.

"I was young once, too, Dakota. And your boyfriend is no slouch."

"Huh?" Had she just call my "boyfriend" hot?

"Honey," she warned, "do I look like an idiot? Just promise you'll be safe, okay?"

"No. It's just that I—"

"Ooh." My mom glanced at her watch. "Gotta go. See you tonight, honey."

"But—" she disappeared.

I lay back in bed and stared at the ceiling. This was all just so dang bizarre, and the gift of a full night of sleep hadn't changed that one bit.

"Nice pajamas."

I popped up on my elbows.

Santiago's intimidating, well-muscled frame occupied the doorway. He wore black leather boots, a navy blue tee, and faded button flies that hugged his powerful legs. I didn't want to acknowledge how looking at him made me feel things I had no business feeling. But that would be like trying to ignore a truck parked on your face.

He bowed his head. "Good morning, Dakota," he said in that deep, almost too-masculine-to-be-true voice with the thick Spanish accent.

"I...I..."

"We're back to stuttering again, are we?"

I nodded, and he smiled as if I amused him.

"Get dressed—I have business to take care of today, so you'll be going to my place after you eat."

He had a place? "Your place?"

"Yes."

"Why am I going there?"

Anger flickered in his eyes. "Because I can't leave you here alone. My house is..." he paused, carefully considering his words, "in the hills, about fifteen minutes from here."

"I don't understand."

"Don't understand what?" he asked.

"Why you think I'd leave here and go anywhere with you?"

"Thought I'd answered that question already. Only, I'll add to it that if you don't come willingly, I'll drag you. Get dressed." He left and closed the door behind him.

Oh crap. I didn't want to go anywhere with him. What if his house had a basement with my name on it? And would he really drag me out of my home, kicking and screaming? No. Something told me this guy didn't want to be noticed. He lived in the shadows.

A ghost...

I decided that no matter what, staying in my pajamas was not going to be helpful. I threw on my favorite jeans and a tee and then pulled my hair back into a ponytail.

Suddenly, I heard a loud crash from somewhere inside the house. I placed my ear to my bedroom door. The ruckus continued. Then I heard grunting and an "Ahhh!"

I yanked open the door and went into the hallway. The sound was actually coming from my mother's bedroom only two doors down.

I ran and looked inside, hoping and praying it wasn't my mother making that awful sound.

"Oh my God!" I screamed. Santiago was on top of a man, pounding him in the face. I couldn't see the guy well, but he appeared to be wearing some sort of blue work uniform, like those guys from the electric company.

Santiago looked up at me. "Go to your room and lock the door. Don't come out until I get you," he screamed.

I couldn't move.

"Do it!" he commanded.

I found my legs and scrambled to my bedroom, locking the door behind me. As an extra measure, I went into my private bathroom and locked that door, too. The house fell into an eerie silence, and I vacillated between holding my breath and panting. I could only imagine what was happening. Santiago was going to kill the man, right there in my mother's bedroom.

Oh my God. What do I do?

Several minutes passed before I womaned up, went back into my room, and grabbed my phone next to my bed. I was about to hit 911 when I heard the sirens. I looked out my window at the two police cars pulling up. Had the neighbors heard the noise?

Thank God.

Deep voices rumbled through the house, and I wondered if they were taking Santiago away along with whomever he'd been beating to death. One could only hope.

What felt like an hour passed before a light knock on the door startled me from my state of paralysis. "Dakota. It's safe now," came Santiago's deep voice. He knocked again. "Dakota? Open up."

I slowly unlocked the door and turned the handle, cracking open the door.

Santiago's intense gaze greeted me. "The police are here," he said. "They want to speak to you."

"What happened?" I asked.

"Some asshole burglar. Nothing to be afraid of," he replied.

"What? Someone just broke into my house?" I asked.

"Yeah. Thankfully," he mumbled.

"I'm not following. You're happy someone tried to rob us while I was home?"

He shrugged. "Come on. The police are waiting." Santiago marched downstairs, and I followed. The living room, a sort of ode-to-white shrine because my mother liked to meditate in there, crawled with uniformed people.

"Hello Dakota, I'm officer Melrose," said the shorter, blond policeman.

I shook his hand.

"I understand you're not feeling well after yesterday's little incident, so Santiago's asked that we don't take much of your time," he said. "Can you tell me what you saw?"

Santiago's asked? Since when were the police so accommodating?

Santiago moved to my side and placed his arm around me. "It's okay, Dakota. Don't be afraid," he whispered in my ear.

Afraid? I was so frenetic I thought I might actually pee myself. "I—I—heard a crash and then saw Santiago beating some man in my mother's bedroom," I managed to eke out.

"Thank you, that's all I need," the officer said.

I was about to throw myself at the officer's mercy, beg him to help me, when he turned to Santiago. "Can't thank you enough for catching this guy. He fits the description of someone who's wanted for rape, murder, and ten counts of burglary."

"Rape? Murder?" I blurted out.

"A woman walked in on him while he was cleaning her out," said the officer.

How horrible. Could that have been me?

"No problem," Santiago said. "Thanks for showing up so quickly."

"That's what we're here for," Officer Melrose said. "After yesterday, I hate to ask you to come in again, but will Monday work to make a formal statement?"

So they already knew Santiago because he'd been to the station after Janice ran me over.

"No problem. Thanks." Santiago shook his hand.

Officer Melrose looked at me. "You've got a really good guy there, Dakota. I'd hang on to that one."

I stood there completely flabbergasted as the officers left the house.

Santiago's phone rang, and he quickly answered it. "Yeah?" He listened for a few moments. "No." He listened some more. "Of course." He hung up the phone.

"What the hell just happened?" I asked. And who was he speaking to?

"You got lucky. That's what happened," he replied.

"Some guy broke in and my stalker—who's holding me prisoner, by the way—happened to catch him and beat the crap out of him. Not sure I'd call that luck."

Santiago brushed his hand through his messy, dark hair, and I couldn't help noticing how his generous biceps flexed as he did this.

I'm an idiot.

"My mother was killed by an intruder," he said matter-of-factly. "I found her facedown on the kitchen floor when I was ten. So, yeah, I call it luck."

I gasped. "That's awful. I'm so sorry."

He shrugged. "So am I. They never caught the guy."

What a tragic story. I couldn't imagine how he felt, never getting justice for something like that. I wondered if that had something to do with why he was with me; however, when I jammed the clue in with the other pieces, the puzzle remained scrambled. He had a past, a tormented one that haunted him. Still didn't explain why he was invading my life or threatening me not to squeal.

Suddenly, my stomach lurched, and I felt my legs giving out. Santiago caught me before I hit the floor.

He scooped me up in his arms, and though I didn't black out, the dizziness and pounding in my head made it impossible to open my eyes. He held me tightly and carried me up the stairs. I heard the pounding of Santiago's heart against his chest, and I felt the warmth of his body against mine. I couldn't deny it felt strangely comforting. Yes, he was real. He had to be. Ghosts didn't have heartbeats and radiate heat. Ghosts didn't get phone calls or casually speak of their dead mothers.

"You're all right, Dakota," he whispered. "I won't let anyone hurt you."

Had he meant me to hear that? Or did he think I was out cold?

I remained perfectly still, hoping he might reveal something more, another piece of the puzzle.

He laid me down on my bed and ran his hand over my face before checking my pulse. "You're strong, Dakota. Just like I knew you would be."

He knew I would be? Like he'd been planning to meet me? But I'd randomly found his picture.

Then I felt something I didn't expect. His lips brushed across my cheek. And while I didn't want to admit it, something about the gentleness sent tiny waves of pinpricks charging through my entire body. I felt like I'd been licked by a hungry, dangerous lion. It felt fucking wonderful.

I gasped and opened my eyes. Santiago immediately straightened up, startled by my abrupt awakening.

He stared at my face for a moment, studying me with what could only be interpreted as some sort of admiration. Then, as if catching himself doing something he shouldn't, he started to turn away. "You haven't eaten yet; I'll be back with those pancakes I made you. Then we're leaving."

He made me pancakes? This was all too much. Too bizarre. He threatened me, protected me, made me breakfast. He watched over me like an overzealous boyfriend.

"Wait!" I sat up, and I could see from the look on his face that his patience was being tried. "Please, whatever is going on, whatever is happening, I need to know."

"Know what?" he growled.

"Who are you?"

His fists clenched into tight little balls. "I told you, stop asking."

I held out my palms. "I don't know what's happened or what I've done to you—I mean, yes, I stole your photo—and I'm sorry—but other than that, I have no clue what this is all about. Please, just tell me."

He marched over and glared down before placing both hands on the sides of my face. The kinder, gentler Santiago I'd seen only moments ago was nowhere to be found. "Do you want your mother to get hurt, Dakota? Do you?" He pulled back but kept a firm grip on my face. "Because if you do, keep asking questions you know I won't answer. Keep resisting."

I stared at his face and saw something in the depths of those dark, sultry eyes. A sort of sadness or, perhaps, fear.

"Do you want someone to die, Dakota?" he whispered coldly.

My body instantly reacted to his brutal words, but my mind screeched to a halt. He had made it sound like he would do the hurting, but now I knew that just couldn't be right. Could it? So did that mean someone else wanted to hurt me and my mother?

"Answer me," he said.

I shook my head no.

"Then, who am I?"

"My boyfriend," I croaked.

"Very good." He released his grip. "And you will stop asking questions?"

I couldn't promise that so I didn't respond.

His eyes narrowed just a bit. "Dakota," he blew out a tension-filled breath, and I could've sworn I saw steam. "Is what I'm asking you to do so terrible? Is it so hard to imagine me being your boyfriend—a guy who will make sure nothing bad ever happens to you again? Who will do everything possible to make sure you live a long, happy life?" He inclined his head and whispered in my ear. "Is it so hard to pretend that you're mine?"

The narrow space of air between us filled with a strange tension. If I didn't know any better, I would say it was sexual. My stomach fluttered and breasts began to tingle. My heart felt like it might beat its way out of my chest. I suddenly couldn't stop thinking about his full lips. What would he taste like? I wondered.

Crap? What's wrong with me? My mind caught up with my very gullible body, realizing that he had switched tactics on me. Intimidation no longer did the trick so now he was using my obvious sexual attraction to him to kowtow me. The sad part was, it almost worked, and that was the irony of the situation. He scared me. And the more frightened I felt, the more drawn to him I became. It was as if he could sense it, too, because he had no problem tuning right in and using his body and voice to make me feel like he really wanted me.

Idiot. He's playing you.

"Are you going to hurt me or my mother?"

"I would die for either one of you. In a heartbeat. "

That wasn't the answer I expected. Why would he say something so morbid and dramatic? "How am I supposed to believe a word you say when you keep threatening us?"

He shook his head. "You don't need to believe my words, just look at my actions."

His actions said I should be very, very afraid of him. He was lethal, sexy, and a complete enigma. But something in my gut made me want to believe him. Perhaps it was that tormented look in his eyes. I just didn't know.

"Can you at least tell me something about yourself? Do you have more family? Where do they live? Do you have a brother, dog, fish? Tell me anything so I know you're real."

He stared for a sobering moment, his beautiful brown eyes as cold as a slab of granite. "I like camping."

"What?"

"You know, camping. Trees. Mountains. Cooking over a fire."

This was not the sort of personal information I'd meant. "Does your version of camping involve a gun and killing something?"

He shrugged his brows. "A man's gotta eat."

"Figures."

"You asked for something personal. I gave it." He crossed his thick, muscular arms over his chest.

"Yes, you did."

"Now you'll stop asking questions?" he said.

I hung my head, thinking the worst of my faculties. A small part of me wanted to play nice and stop resisting the situation. "I'm crazy. I have to be."

He sat next to me on the bed and placed his hand on my leg. "You are not crazy," he grumbled. "There is a logical explanation for everything."

I looked into his eyes and was hit with a rush of adrenaline. Simply sitting so close, sharing his space, and gazing into his eyes felt dangerous. And I couldn't deny it sucked me in. I imagined it was how wolves felt about their alphas. They were attracted to the alphas' savage recklessness—their power, their innate ability to do as they pleased without fear of consequence. A part of me wanted to follow.

"Better?" he asked.

Of course I wasn't. Regardless, I pressed my lips together and nodded.

"Good." He stood up. "Then I have your commitment to stop the infantile tactics?"

I nodded. "Okay."

"Then we're on the same page."

"If your page is a flaming ball of devastating terror, then yes. We are absolutely on the same page."

"I know this isn't easy, Dakota, but this will all be over quickly. If you do as I say," he added.

"Really?" *Because I might do just about anything to make this nightmare go away.*

He grinned, and I wondered if it was because he'd found the secret key to gaining my compliance. "Yes."

"How long?" I asked.

"Perhaps a few more days. Perhaps a few weeks."

"I'm not going to your house or anywhere alone with you," I blurted out.

He growled something under his breath. "It's not sa—" Again, he stopped himself.

"I don't feel well," I pushed. "I need to stay here and rest."

He tilted his head and scratched the black stubble on his jaw.

My cell rang on my nightstand, and I practically dove for it. It was my mother. "Hi, Mom."

"I just heard. Why didn't you call me? Are you all right?" she asked, frantic and panting.

"Fine. I'm completely fine. I promise."

I heard her let out a slow breath. "Thank God Santiago was there."

I looked at Santiago, who now stood like a sentinel, arms crossed again. "Yeah," I replied. "Lucky me. Are you coming home?"

"There was an accident on the freeway; they're bringing in fifteen people, and we're down two nurses today. Can you hang tight for another few hours? Santiago can stay with you until I get there, right?"

Ugh. "No, Mom. Don't come home. I'm fine. Really." *Not really. Please come home*, my tone said.

She hesitated for a moment. "All right. But if you change your mind, call me." Sirens soared in the background. "I gotta go, baby. I love you."

I put down the phone and sighed. I was on my own, I realized. I needed to take control.

"If you really mean it," I said, "if you're not here to hurt me, then prove it. Back off. Let me stay home here where I feel safe."

He sucked in a deep, slow breath almost as if he didn't have the will to continue arguing. "I'm warning you, Dakota, I'll be keeping an eye on you, so don't leave this house. Don't do anything stupid. And if you run, I'll find you. If you run, there will be consequences. For everyone. I'll pick you up on Monday for school."

"Why do you have to pick me up?"

"I promised your mother. She doesn't want you driving just yet." He turned to leave.

"Thank you, Santiago," I blurted out, surprised by my own unexpected burst of gratitude. "Thank you for stopping that lunatic who broke in."

He nodded and stalked from the room, leaving me alone, swimming in my own desperate thoughts.

CHAPTER ELEVEN

Monday.

Confined to my house and turning down several shopping invitations via text from Mandy, I spent the weekend arriving at three very important, rational conclusions.

One: If Santiago wanted to harm me, he would have done so by now. No, that didn't mean I trusted him, but I didn't feel as petrified as I probably should have. In any case, once fear is removed from a situation, it does allow you to see things differently, which leads to my next point.

Two: When something generally doesn't make sense, it's because you don't have all the facts. So that's what I began doing, looking for facts, answers. But Santiago Asturias was a ghost. I'd found hundreds of people with the same name, but not *the* Santiago Asturias. Maybe that wasn't his real name. After all, I'd invented that, too. What I found odd, however, was being unable to find the website from where I'd nabbed his photo. There was no trace of this man anywhere: Facebook, Twitter, LinkedIn, Google Images. *Nada*.

Three: I was on my own. My mother had stayed at the hospital the entire weekend due to yet another shortage of nurses, and my father's phone was turned off. Voicemail only. And strangely, each time I tried to call someone other than my parents, the signals on both my cell and landline went all screechy. When I dared to look outside, there was Santiago. At one point, maybe out of boredom, I actually saw the guy mowing the front lawn and trimming the trees. Strange, to say the least.

So basically, that left me confined to the house with nothing but the train wreck inside my head. Why was Santiago here? What did he really want? When would he leave? Was he, perhaps, a real, live ghost? Someone I'd brought to life by speaking him into existence?

No, I supposed he wasn't a ghost who enjoyed gardening, but everything was beyond bizarre. There had to be a logical explanation. Even he had said so.

I gulped down my coffee, looked at my watch, and yawned loudly. It was almost 8:00 a.m., the time I'd normally leave for school, and time to face my "ghost."

I yawned again. How would I make it through the day without falling asleep? I'd tossed and turned for hours last night after having the most intense, vivid dream. The sort that made me blush when I woke up. Obviously, the man was brutally attractive. I'd have to be dead or in a coma not to notice Santiago's raw masculinity—his powerful body, fierce gaze, and fearless posture. But why in the world had I dreamt about baking cookies with him? Well, it started out that way. But then we were naked and covered in cookie batter, which led to us being in the shower. Before I knew it, I was washing his wet, hard body, touching and exploring every steely inch of him. And there were many, many inches. But strangely, he never really moved or touched me back. He simply gazed at me with hungry eyes, as if I were some kind of forbidden fruit he wanted to devour. Even when I took my soap-slick hands and began stroking him, he simply stared right up until the very end when he closed his eyes and screamed my name, rocking himself frantically into my hands. That's when I woke up a hot mess.

Needless to say, my body was in no mood for sleep after that. It was in the mood for something else.

"Don't think about it," I'd told myself, ashamed for having such incredibly lustful fantasies at a time like this. But when I closed my eyes and tried to return to sleep, I saw those images of his tanned, muscular body straining against my hand. That's when I got out my journal and tried to purge the sinful thoughts. But writing them down only made the dream more real, only made me sweat. Before I knew it, it was morning and time for a shower. A cold, cold shower.

I didn't want him. Did I? He was an icy, scary enigma. Maybe that was it. A sick little part of me enjoyed the danger he represented to my sad, tame, wallflower of a life.

Idiot.

The doorbell rang, and I jumped out of my flip-flops, nearly landing on my butt.

Crap. He's here.

I ran my trembling hands over my smoothed-back hair, trapped neatly into a bun, and then tugged on the front of my tight baby-blue tee. I took in a breath and yanked open the door.

And release breath.

Santiago stood on the porch, one hand shoved into the pocket of his faded button flies, his white T-shirt stretching across his unfathomably muscled chest and upper biceps, his black hair a hot mess. *Just like my night.*

Dark shades covered his dark eyes, but I could've sworn he was checking out my breasts and midriff. My T-shirt suddenly felt too small. I gave it another tug, trying to close the gap between the bottom hem and the top of my low-rise, vintage Levis.

He jerked his head. "Ready?"

No. Not at all. The guy dripped with danger. And anger. And sensuality.

I swiped my backpack and stepped out, closing the door behind me. When my eyes hit the curb, I stopped. "That's your ride?"

Not that I expected him to take me to school on a motorcycle, but his other vehicle wasn't what one might think. Not a muscle car—Mustang or Camaro. Not a race car—Porsche, Ferrari, Lamborghini. Not a yuppie car—BMW, Mercedes, Lexus. But a big red Bronco. An old one. No top. Just a steering wheel, black seats, a roll bar, and fat tires. The kind of truck you hoped you never had to get into while wearing a tight skirt.

"I guess that explains the hair," I said.

He grumbled something about classics under his breath and stepped aside as I passed.

When he grabbed my hand and helped me fumble my way into the vehicle, my body lit up like a bonfire. It remembered touching his skin, and it didn't care if the memories were fictional, a dream. My body simply wanted to have another taste. Muscles tightened. Nerves tingled. Saliva flowed. He was like a giant danger-brownie and my body wanted a big fat bite.

Crap, Dakota. Get a hold of yourself.

I watched him walk around the front of the truck, his backside moving like two impenetrable cannonball halves under the soft denim fabric of his jeans. *Don't. Don't think about the dream.* I pushed away the images still fresh in my mind.

"Stop looking at my ass," he barked without bothering to look in my direction.

"I was looking at the…" *Shit.* "Windshield wipers. You should try changing them once in a while."

"Changed them yesterday. Stop staring at my fucking ass. You're too young for me."

What? How crude. Why had he blurted that out? It was so strange and out of context. "Thank God for that."

With his enormous stature, he easily slipped into the driver's seat. "I'm not your toy. We won't be having sex."

"Who said I wanted to?" I retorted with disgust.

Your dreams said you wanted to.

Shut up!

He shoved the key into the ignition and twisted. "I'm not making out with you either. I don't believe in any form of intimate contact with a minor."

Where had all this come from? "First off, I'm eighteen. Second, I never asked you to touch me—I happen to like guys who are human. And third, I didn't even ask you into my life."

"Right." He shifted into first and released the clutch. "Then why the hell am I here, Dakota?"

Ummm…"Damned good question."

"Don't start," he grumbled over the loud engine.

"Grumpy much? If all that phone hacking puts you in such a bad mood, maybe you shouldn't do it," I spouted back.

He completely ignored my hacking comment and mumbled something about not getting any sleep for several days because *someone* had insisted on staying at her house. I guessed that someone was me. And I guessed that meant he *had* been camped outside my house the entire weekend, as I suspected.

"You could've come inside and taken a nap on the couch," I said as we pulled up to a stop sign.

Why did I say that? And why did I find myself wishing he had?

He gazed at me from behind those black lenses. "Trust me," he replied in a deep, slow voice, "I wanted to." He looked ahead. "But you needed your rest. Although, you don't seem to get much."

I wasn't sure what he meant, but I was sure he hadn't intended his response to sound loaded with sexual innuendo, which is exactly how my body interpreted it. My heart began to accelerate and my belly filled with prickles.

Wait. He's doing that sexual power play thing to me again. Regardless, I couldn't deny it had an effect. My body was simply all too willing to play along, to play with him.

I smiled, masking my inappropriate thoughts. "Well, thank you. Because I slept like a baby." Obviously, I hadn't, but he didn't know that. Or maybe he did if he'd been watching me. My bedroom light had been on all night.

Regardless, he didn't reply.

Minutes later, Santiago's truck roared into the school parking lot, our awkward silence a contrast to the obnoxious, vintage muscle truck.

"Why are you parking?" I asked.

He put the truck into neutral, pulled the brake, and turned off the engine. "I'm taking you to class. What the hell does it look like?"

He hopped out and walked around to my side.

"C'mon." He held out his arms as if he were going to catch me like a toddler jumping from the swings at the park.

I frowned. "Back off."

He grumbled and did as I asked.

Only a narrow space separated our bodies as I slid from the truck, and I could've sworn he radiated some sort of sexual energy, because my body reacted instantly: goose bumps, neck hair standing at full attention, girl parts begging me to zero in on their target, commanding my eyes to seek out his…well, boy parts.

He removed his glasses and stared with that penetrating gaze as I inched away from him, my back against the vehicle. I could only hope he wasn't noticing my physical reaction.

"You're not even a student here," I said. "You can't come with me."

He laughed. "Like some fucking rules would ever stop me." He caught my arm, leaned in, and whispered in my ear. He seemed to do that a lot. Was it because he knew it instantly got my attention? "I can go anywhere I like, Dakota. There are no walls, no laws, no school rules that can stop me."

I shivered as I felt his hot breath tickle my skin. "What can? What will stop you?" I murmured, never expecting him to answer.

"An itch," he replied.

An itch? "An itch?"

He breathed into my ear, and I inhaled deeply. He smelled like male. Cinnamon, testosterone. Male. "We all have needs. Sometimes those needs can't be ignored." His lips brushed across my cheek and stopped at the corner of my mouth. "Sometimes…we have to scratch."

Unable to keep myself from remembering the dream and every hot, hard inch of him, my body tensed. But there was no doubt in my mind he was toying with me, trying to rattle my cage. But why? What had I done?

I tilted my head to the side. "You should have that itch looked at. Maybe you caught something."

He laughed into the air.

I took advantage and scurried away like a little rodent fleeing from the light. "I can get to class on my own."

He jerked his head. "Don't be late, babe. I'll see you at lunch."

I flashed several glances over my shoulder until I rounded the corner and he was out of sight.

What had brought about this sudden change in him? Because this felt like more than a simple mind game used to keep me in check. The tension he radiated felt intense, real. It was as if he knew my mind had been in the gutter all night, and he was all too happy to join me. But my dreams were just that. Dreams. I couldn't control them, and I certainly wasn't about to give into them. No way.

Then it suddenly dawned on me. I was free. He couldn't keep an eye on me here. To hell with what I'd promised. I had to tell someone what was happening, even if they thought I was crazy. But would they? *No. Not possible.* I would go to the principal's office, and have her call the police. No one was above the law, and this entire thing had gotten out of hand. I was dangerously close to accepting the situation, believing it, and wanting things I had no business wanting.

Stockholm syndrome.

But what about his warning that someone would get hurt? Or his threat about telling my mom? Okay. I didn't believe he would hurt me. And I didn't believe there was some ominous force coming after me. That was ridiculous, likely a ploy to keep me quiet. But the part about my mom? If Santiago told her about my dad cheating, it would tear her to pieces.

Shit. I thought about it for a moment, and realized that the real reason I didn't want Santiago to tell her wasn't because I feared her learning the truth, it was because I'd never said a word. I felt like I was the one who'd betrayed her, not my father.

So there it was. My answer. My father needed to fix this. He needed to help me. He needed to tell my mother the truth. That would free me from Santiago and my guilt. It would restore a tiny piece of my respect for him.

I'd left several messages for my father over the weekend, but he hadn't called back. Why? And he'd completely flaked on our FaceTime date.

Time to try him again.

I started digging into my purse for my phone. *Damn it.* I'd left it charging on my desk. I quickly thought about hunting down Mandy, but her phone didn't have international access. I could, however, use the phone in the office—tell them it was a family emergency.

As I turned the corner, down the crowded corridor toward the administrative building, the sane thoughts in my head evaporated. Every student stopped or moved to let me pass. They shamelessly whispered and gawked in my general direction, parting like the Red Sea as I passed.

I ran my hand over the top of my head. Did I look horrible? The bruise *was* pretty bad.

But then the students began to applaud and cheer, "Fuck yeah!" and "Ding dong the witch is dead!" They roared like a crowd at a football game. I suddenly realized I was in front of my homeroom and ducked inside, out of sight.

The strange behavior, unfortunately, didn't stop there. Steve, the captain of the football team, immediately held out his palm. "Dakota! Put 'er there, woman."

In shock, I stretched out my hand, and he slapped it so hard that my skin stung from the impact. As everyone poured in, they saluted, patted, and hugged me until the bell rang. Everyone except Dax, who watched from his seat in the corner, his expression somewhat pensive, as if he were staring at a zoo creature. When the teacher entered, it wasn't Mr. M but a substitute who immediately made threats of detention if people didn't calm down.

I sank into my chair toward the back, fighting the urge to vomit. Had the universe tilted itself on its head and shifted its polar axis? Why were people being so nice?

Head spinning with confusion, I didn't hear one bit of the lecture. As soon as the bell rang, I popped up from my seat and bolted for the door. I rounded the corner to the main office and skidded to a halt, nearly getting trampled by some girls behind me.

Santiago?

He stood in front of the admin building with the principal, Ms. Marie. She giggled, her eyes glued to Santiago's bulging biceps as he spoke. They didn't look like they were going to stop talking anytime soon either.

Damn it. Ms. Marie was the only one who had the code for long distance calls. I knew this because my mom had forgotten a field trip permission slip last year. When I called her at work to see if she could fax it over, they told me she was tied up. I tried to call my dad next, but the call wouldn't go through until Ms. Marie punched in the code.

I ground my teeth. How was it possible? Santiago had everyone wrapped around his little finger. My mother, my best friend; now the principal. Even the police and people at the hospital seemed to be under his spell.

I went to class to bide my time. If I couldn't get to a phone during school, then I'd call my dad when I got home. And I knew my father wouldn't be so easily manipulated by Santiago's charms. As much as I had trust issues with the man, he was ruthless when it came to stuff like people messing with his family. Once, I remember my mother had an issue with a new doctor at work. He kept hitting on her or something. I knew she'd tried to talk to the doctor to get him to stop, but when she did, he threatened to have her fired if she complained to HR. My mother finally gave in and told my father. Not only did the doctor never bother her again, he lost his license and left the state. I knew my mom felt kind of bad, but I didn't. Jerk had probably been harassing poor nurses for years. I only wish I knew what my dad said to send the guy fleeing for his life. Must've been pretty damned entertaining, because my dad was scary. He always knew the exact pressure points to maximize fear. That's why I had to believe he'd know what to do. He always knew what to do.

༔

By lunch I was suffering from severely low blood sugar, and the dizzy spells were growing stronger. I'd been so nerve-racked in the morning because of Santiago coming to pick me up that I hadn't eaten. I definitely needed food.

Ignoring the other students' gawks, I stood in line with my tray: a slice of greasy pizza, red Jell-O, and orange slices. I neared the register and felt a very deliberate push from behind. "Bitch!"

The contents of the tray went flying, as did I. My body slammed onto the cold tile floor, sending the air whooshing from my lungs. I immediately heard grunting and a guy behind me scream.

I rolled onto my back to see Santiago gripping the boy—only he wasn't really a boy, but a mannish teen with a beard, BO, wide shoulders in a letterman jacket—by the collar of his shirt. His name was Jer. Mr. Dipshit Quarterback. It was a widely known fact he worshipped Janice.

"Get the fuck off me, dude!" Jer struggled, but Santiago whipped him around like a tiny rag doll, threw him facedown on the floor, and placed his thick boot in the small of Jer's back. Santiago kneeled and grabbed Jer's hand, twisting his wrist and placing him in some weird pretzel hold.

"Don't ever fucking touch her again. Do you hear me?" Santiago said in a low, menacing voice. "I know where you live, where you eat, I know where you piss. None of which you'll ever do again if you lay another fucking finger on her."

The entire cafeteria fell into a horrified hush as everyone froze in their tracks, including the register lady.

My eyes practically did somersaults out of my head. *Oh no!* "Let him go, Santiago. You're going to break his arm."

"Say you heard me, asshole," Santiago was as cool as a lethal cucumber, and ignored me.

"I heard you." Jer's bright red face was smushed against the dirty floor as he managed to form the words.

"You'll never touch her again," Santiago whispered. "Right?"

"Right."

Santiago released Jer's hand, slid his booted foot to the floor, and looked at me. "You! Outside."

I pointed at myself. "Me?" *Oh no.* I wasn't going anywhere with this madman.

Just then, Ms. Marie showed up. Her eyes zeroed in on Jer, who was picking himself and his very battered ego up off the floor. "Mr. Jerold Parker! To my office!"

Jer pointed at Santiago, who simply nodded his head to greet the principal. "But this guy just—"

Ms. Marie pointed to the exit. "Office! Now!"

Jer did as he was told, clearly baffled by the situation.

"I'm so sorry, Mr. Asturias," Ms. Marie groveled, grinning goofily before returning to her frown and trailing behind Jer.

Santiago's lethal gaze shifted back to me, and the entire lunchroom continued to stare in silence.

"You. Outside. Now," he growled.

Oh my God, he was going to kill me and no one was going to stop him.

I turned slowly and walked outside, listening to the students' voices explode as we left. I suddenly felt the urge to run and never look back. Instead, I walked at a brisk pace, weighing self-defense options.

"Where the hell do you think you're going, Dakota?"

I didn't answer, but headed for the parking lot.

"Dakota…" he warned.

"Stop! Okay! Just stop!" I turned, and he almost rammed right into me. "You are not my father. Don't tell me what to do. I don't even know who the—"

He moved so fast that I didn't even see him coming. He cupped his hand over my mouth and pulled me into him. "Don't. Don't say another word."

Though he towered over me, his dark eyes were inches from mine, his anger palpable. But I didn't feel afraid. Not even close. I felt…riled up. Then I noticed the heat from his body, the hardness of his chest against mine, and the feeling

66

of his hips pressed against me. They only made me think about one ridiculous thing. Sex.

Damned you, stupid hormones!

Well, my brain was stronger than my hormones, and my rational thought wouldn't be overridden by some ridiculous, biological response to this man's body. And face. And…*everything*.

"You're making a scene, and everyone is watching," he seethed. "You will calm yourself. You will remember everything I told you. And you will never challenge me again. Nod if you understand."

I nodded, but only so he'd let go.

"I'm going to release you now. I'm trusting you." He slid his hand from my face, and I immediately opened my mouth to scream at him. But before any sound made it past my lips, he covered my mouth with his.

His lips were hard and soft and *hot*. All in one. He pulled me closer, and though a part of me really, really wondered why he was kissing me, the other part was too busy noticing the roughness of his stubble scraping the edges of my lips as his hot mouth worked over mine. That other part of me also noticed the heat explode from every point of contact between our two bodies. It noticed his strong hands pushed into the small of my back, pressing me to him like a vice. Damn it. The man tasted like fifty-one flavors of sin—sweet, salty, sexy—and I wanted more.

I slid my hands around his neck and deepened the kiss. His tongue thrust against mine in a blatant erotic rhythm that sparked an unexpected groan from somewhere deep inside my chest. He returned the groan and upped the ante with a hard, heated object pressed against my belly.

"Christ!" He suddenly pulled his head back. A look of sheer shock danced in his eyes before being replaced with an icy, controlled glare.

Wow. What was that? Another ploy to control me? Or had what I just felt been as real as my body told me it was?

"Why did you do that?" he growled.

I dropped my arms. "Wait. You kissed me."

He stepped back and ran his hands through his messy black hair. "Only to shut you up."

"You could've just used your hand again," I panted.

He glowered, and I noticed the vein pulsing in his neck. "Damn it," he seethed under his breath. "I—fuck. Fuck…" He lowered his head and blew out a loud breath. "I thought you were—and then I—shit, never mind. Just get your ass back to class and stay out of trouble." He turned away.

I never imagined it could happen, not with this man, but Santiago was visibly shaken. "What the hell is the matter with you?"

Santiago was right back in my face again. "You have no idea what you're messing with, do you?"

Hello? Ummm…that would be a big fat, no! "All I know is that I was hit by a car, you appeared in my life, and now I'm your prisoner." *And you just kissed the breath out of me in the school parking lot.*

"You forgot the part," he seethed quietly, "about how someone broke into your house, and you'd be dead right now if it weren't for me. But if that's not enough to entice you to stop challenging me, then maybe I should have a talk with your mother."

Maybe I should tell him I don't care anymore. I only hoped he wouldn't find something else to blackmail me with. He seemed like the type of man who had many tricks up his sleeve. That kiss, for example. But what else could he use against me? Apart from my family and Mandy, there was only one other thing that mattered. High school. As in, getting out of it.

Oh no.

"W…what did you say to Ms. Marie?" I asked. "Why were you in her office?"

His lips formed a sly smile. "Can't talk about it. Official business."

He'd told her he was someone "official"? And she believed him? "So what did you say? Are you trying to fuck up my chances for college? Get me expelled or something?"

His nostrils flared, and his hands tightened into fists. "I would never do that to you."

"Oh. But you'd threaten to hurt me and break up my family?"

"I never threatened to hurt you," he growled.

"Like hell you didn't." At the very least, he'd said things that led me to believe they were physical threats. And he hadn't denied trying to break up my family.

"You're a fucking psycho." I stepped forward, chin lifted.

"And you're a spoiled little brat." Chest heaving, he closed the gap between us, pressing his body against mine.

Then I felt it again. That tension. The heat. Being near him caused an instant chemical reaction in my brain. I wanted to claw at his clothes and taste those lips again.

He began to lower his head, but then his beautiful dark eyes narrowed, and his jaw muscles pulsed with agitation. "Get your ass to your next class, Dakota. I'll pick you up right here."

My body in complete shambles, I backed away. Because despite everything my brain told me, this man completely undid me.

Get a hold of yourself, Dakota. He's just using your lust to control you. Yes, it was no secret the man was built like a god. By now, he had to know his body was his most powerful weapon against my young, overly eager, hormone-riddled body. I just needed to bide a little time, make it home, and call my dad. He would know what to do. He would fix this.

I walked off to class, holding in that scream still begging me to let it loose.

༄༄

The rest of my classes were a blur. I felt too scared and in too much shock to pay any attention to the other students who kept hounding me during the breaks. Some asked about Janice, others about Santiago. When I finally saw Mandy right before my final class, I almost collapsed at her feet and kissed her toes. I opted for hugging her instead.

"Where have you been?" I asked.

"I had a dentist appointment. Got here after lunch. Why?" She smiled brightly. In her pink T-shirt dress and flip-flops she looked bound for the beach.

Oh no! The senior party. "Is the pool party today?"

Disappointment flooded her eyes. "You forgot, didn't you?"

Mandy had signed up for decorations and made me promise to go. With everything that had happened, it had slipped my mind.

"It's okay. I understand," she said, squeezing my arm. "After all, you were hit by a car, hospitalized, someone broke into your house, and—by the way, is it true your boyfriend showed up and kicked the crap out of Jer?"

I nodded.

"I really, really like your boyfriend. Do you know how many times Jer has spit on me?"

"Hey, Dakota." Dax stood there with a goofy grin on his face. He wore an orange logo shirt and Hawaiian-style board shorts. I immediately noticed how, before, he'd always seemed so huge, larger than life. But now, he looked so boyish and innocent. Did he even shave?

What the hell's happened to me?

"Hi," I said.

"You going after school?" he asked.

"To the pool party?" I wasn't going anywhere, and I might never be free again. But why did he want to know?

"I'm going! I helped with the decorations," Mandy offered.

Dax stared at me waiting for an answer, completely ignoring her. *Jerk.*

"Can't." I pointed to my bruised face. "Doctor said I need to take it easy for another week."

"Oh. Well, let me know when you're feeling better. Maybe we'll hang out."

Wait. Wasn't he afraid of my psycho stalker? I didn't know if I should give him a point for bravery or deduct one for stupidity.

I smiled. Not too big. "Sure."

Dax strolled away, and Mandy's face lit up. "He likes you!" she squealed.

Yeah, well, I wasn't the least bit interested in him anymore. Besides, even if I were, what good would it do me now? I was the prisoner of a man I'd made up.

CHAPTER TWELVE

After class, Santiago's truck waited curbside, his predatory eyes watching me from behind dark glasses as I begrudgingly approached. It was an exceptionally hot day, not so atypical for a California spring, but Santiago seemed perfectly at ease taking in the scorching sun. Not a bead of sweat to be found on the man.

Figured. Ghosts don't sweat.

I climbed in and hugged my backpack, hoping it might shield me from the menacing man behind the steering wheel.

"Put your seat belt on," he commanded.

I obeyed, but didn't speak. I just wanted to get home and call my father.

Santiago cranked the key and the loud engine roared to life. As expected, everyone stared with fascination. Even Dax, who was on the way to his car.

Santiago noticed immediately. Then again, he seemed to be constantly scanning everything and everyone around us.

"I think he likes you," Santiago said.

I shrugged.

"Ah. The silent treatment. Probably for the best. That mouth of yours is trouble."

I looked at him, in shock. A hint of a smile dashed across his lips, then he threw the truck into first and floored it out of the lot.

I hadn't realized it before, but I'd been holding my breath from the moment I got in that truck, only releasing it when Santiago turned at the light in the direction of my house. Thank the Lord he wasn't going to drag me away to some remote cabin in the woods.

Oh no! But we are *going to be alone.* That was equally bad.

Minutes later, we pulled into the driveway, and he turned off the engine. "You can have a break and then start your homework. Your mother will be home at eleven."

What a complete jack…

Remember, just call your dad.

"Sure. Whatever."

He opened the front door, and I slid past him and up the stairs to my room.

I shut the door, again holding my breath, praying Santiago wouldn't follow me.

He didn't, and I dove for my cell. I dialed my father, nearly bursting at the seams with hysterics.

The call went right into his voicemail again. *Son of a bitch!*

"Dad," I whispered, holding my shaky hand over my mouth to muffle the sound. "I need to talk to you. It's urgent. Please call me back. Okay? I need you."

I pressed END.

"Everything all right?" Santiago said.

I jumped out of my skin. I hadn't even heard the door creak. It always creaked. The entire house was built like a squeaky wheel. "Where did you come from?"

His brows knitted together. "From downstairs. What are you up to?"

"Huh?"

"You look like you're up to something."

"No. Just…calling my dad," I said.

He stepped inside the room, and I stepped back.

He frowned, perhaps displeased by my aversion to him.

"It won't happen again," he said. "Don't worry."

"What won't happen again?" I hoped he'd meant the scaring me part.

73

"I won't kiss you again. I'm sorry. It was just a reaction. And after last night—" He stopped whatever he was about to say. Now, while I unsuccessfully attempted to purge erotic images of him from my thoughts, I wondered what he'd been up to the previous evening. But, whatever. I couldn't help my thoughts, and I didn't care why he'd kissed me. Or that I was developing some strange, dark obsession with him.

"Fine. Whatever," I said. "Can I just have some space? I have a lot of catch-up homework to do."

He was about to say something else, but instead closed his mouth and bowed his head, granting me my wish. He closed the door behind him, and this time I heard the floor squeak as he went downstairs. How did he turn his stealth on and off like that?

I sank onto my bed and tried not to let the situation overwhelm me. I slid open my nightstand drawer and grabbed my journal. I began to write,

If only I could make him go away. But how? If I made him up, can't I unmake him up? I want my life back. As horrible as it was, it was mine. I knew I wasn't crazy. Now, my life feels over, and I never even got to live it. Maybe I'm not meant to be happy. Maybe it's time to accept that there is no future for losers like me.

I lay down and pulled the covers up. My head hurt from trying to make sense of everything. I didn't have the energy to fight anymore.

഑ഩ

When my mother's voice woke me, it was already nighttime.

I looked at my nightstand, again forgetting I had not yet purchased a replacement clock. "What time is it?" I rubbed my eyes.

"Just after eleven," she replied. "How's the head? How are you feeling?" she asked, turning on the lamp.

I winced. "Okay. I had a headache. I guess I fell asleep."

She ran her hand over my hair and inspected my eyes. "It will take a while for everything to heal. By the way, where's Santiago?" she asked.

"He's not downstairs?"

"Nope," she replied. "Maybe he got tired and went home."

"If I'm lucky, he'll stay there," I blurted out.

"Did you two fight?"

Fight? Fight? If only it were that simple. I didn't know if it was the grogginess or the pent-up desperation, but I suddenly decided that I had to tell her the truth. And if Santiago told her about my father's cheating, then so be it. Sooner or later, someone would tell her—I'd see to that—but I couldn't wait. I couldn't hold on to this any longer.

"Mom, I don't know how to say this, but Santiago is not my boyfriend."

She cocked her head to the side. "You broke up?"

"No. I mean, he was never my boyfriend. He just…*showed up* in my life. I don't know who he is."

She stared at me, and I could tell her mind was working hard. Then her face turned a sick shade of red, and she swallowed before pasting on the fakest smile I'd ever seen.

"How well do we truly know anyone?" she said stiffly. "Relationships are difficult that way. Oh. That's my phone ringing. You should rest."

I hadn't heard her phone.

"Mom, but there's more. He has been—"

"We can finish this in the morning," she said, marching from the room.

So much for telling my mother. And that reaction? It was as if she didn't want to hear one word of what I had to say. *She thinks you're insane, that's why.* What mother in her right mind wanted to confront that?

I seemed cursed to live this nightmare alone.

ॐ

In the early morning, my phone chirped from somewhere under the covers. I fished it out and looked at the screen, hoping it might be my dad. There was still time for him to come clean on his own. And I still had to believe he could help me.

But it wasn't him.

I answered but didn't speak.

"Dakota, I know you're listening," Santiago's carnal voice poured into my ears. I clamped my eyes shut. "You will tell everyone we fought and broke up. That I went home, and you haven't heard from me since."

What was he saying? "I don't understand."

"You heard what I said?" he repeated, irritated.

"Yes, but—"

"That's all I need." A long pause. "And Dakota? You're a smart, beautiful, young woman. Your life isn't over; it's just beginning. Don't forget that."

The call ended, and Santiago was gone. Just like that. Just as quickly and mysteriously as he'd entered my life, he left it. Like a ghost that had never existed. Even his phone number was disconnected. Yes, I tried it. I don't really know why.

Over the week that followed, I stuck to the story he'd told me, and no one seemed to question it. As for my father, he finally called back a few days after Santiago disappeared. He was extremely apologetic for not returning my calls sooner, but said he'd been "out of pocket," somewhere remote. When I tried to bring up his cheating, he cut me off and said that he and my mother were fighting. He wouldn't say about what, other than he'd broken her trust, and she had every right to be angry. In any case, he planned to give her a little space and wouldn't come home until graduation.

We never got the chance to talk about Santiago. Didn't matter, I guess, because life went on. Life became…perfect. Everything I'd ever hoped it would be. On the outside, anyway.

But every night, I dreamed of Santiago. Those dark eyes. That powerful, soul-gripping gaze. That hard body, stacked with thick muscles. And something deep in the pit of my stomach told me this wasn't the end, but simply the beginning of a lifetime waiting for him to return.

PART TWO

Partly Ghostly Skies,
Fifty Percent Chance of
Rabbit Holes

CHAPTER THIRTEEN

Four and a half months later.

"Bye, baby!" My mother squeezed the breath out of me, and then let go quickly. "Oh. I almost forgot." She reached into her oversized purse. "This is for you. Your father said he'll come out to see the campus as soon as he can. Okay?" My mother shoved a large envelop in my hand and then loaded herself into the car, hiding her watering eyes behind extra-large sunglasses.

I smiled. She didn't want me to see her cry. I so loved her.

She sped off like a bank robber, and I waited until her car disappeared from sight until releasing a satisfied breath. *I made it. A new life. Mine.* It felt good. Really good.

I turned toward the modern, yet institutional-style freshman dorms of UC San Diego and beamed appreciatively at the structure. It was simply perfect: open, clean, filled with possibilities.

I know it sounds strange, but a month or so after "the Santiago incident," I realized how it had changed my life in ways I'd never dreamed. Life—my freedom, my future—took on new meaning. I guess that's normal when you lose something and then get it back. In any case, I'd decided that a lawyer was not who I wanted to be. Not when their world was based on man-made rules that could change or be broken by anyone at any time. Laws were meaningless when people like Santiago roamed the planet. Laws wouldn't save me.

So I started reading everything I could about the mind—how it worked, which illnesses caused delusions, the effects of stress—and I realized three things: Santiago had been real, some things in life simply have no explanation, and, most important, I was not crazy.

What it all boiled down to was one simple fact: Everyone remembered him. And strangely enough, I took comfort in knowing that my brain wasn't broken, and that whoever he was, he'd left, never to return. And I didn't need reasons. I needed to forget him, which is why psychology would be my major. I would learn how memories were stored and how to erase them, because, at the end of the day, my memories were the only thing holding me back.

I swiped my shiny new student ID over the access pad and entered the dorms, a veritable scene of chaos—parents and students were shuffling in and out, unloading boxes, saying their good-byes. The lively vibe made me giddy.

With the elevators packed full of suitcases and bodies, I opted for the stairs. Laughter echoed above as two girls lugged their stuff to their rooms.

"Dakota," that dark, familiar voice filled my ears, and I nearly fell on my face, tripping on the stairs.

Shit! I turned in the direction of the sound but found only a wall and an empty stairwell behind me. I shook my head and laughed. "Really, Dakota? Can't you just let him go?"

"Let who go?"

I jumped.

A petite, skinny blond, wearing a pink tank and khaki short shorts stood on the landing above. "Sorry. Didn't mean to scare you."

I looked up. "It's okay. I was only—"

"I get it. Don't say a word. I had to leave my boyfriend behind, too. He went to Florida State." Her face, though stereotypically pretty—perky nose, smooth tan skin, full lips—scrunched up into an unflattering ball of ugly. "I know it's an excuse. He wants to bone other girls. Idiot." She shrugged. "But, whatever. I can't make him love me. And little does he know that in four years, he'll have screwed his way through college and feel like an empty piece of shit. And do you know who he's going to call?"

"Ummm...you?" I said.

"That's right!" She came down a few steps. "And do you know what I'm going to do when he does?"

"Take him back?"

She frowned. "No way! I'm going to say…'Fuck you and the pile of sluts you rode in on. I'm engaged to a doctor who brings me breakfast in bed every morning, knows I'm smart and kind, worships the ground I walk on, and loves me. Enjoy your shit hole of a life, asshole!'"

*Ummm…okay…*I nodded, speechless. This girl had a mouth on her.

"Oops. Sorry. I get a little cranky when I think about it all. I'm Bridget, by the way." She reached out her hand.

"Dakota." I shook her hand and watched her burst into glee.

"Ohmygod! Dakota? Dakota Dane?" She jumped up and down, clapping. "I'm your roommate!"

I tried to hide my fear of all things perky, but I'm pretty certain my wide eyes gave me away. "Wow."

Bridget bounced down the steps and bear-hugged me. For a girl of one hundred and ten pounds, give or take ten pounds, she was pretty damned strong.

"And don't you worry, Dakota." She gripped me by the shoulders. "My mother was a Tri Delta. My sister was a Tri Delta. We're as good as in."

Had I said anything about pledging a sorority? I didn't remember saying anything. "Thanks."

She raised her shoulders and whooshed out a happy little breath. "Well, roomie. See you upstairs. I have a few more boxes to grab."

"Do you need help?" I asked.

"Nope! Gettin' my workout!"

"Okay." I waved her off, and she skipped her merry way down the stairs.

Great. I have the happiest person on the planet as my roommate.

I entered my dorm room, and though it had only been five minutes max since I'd left it, Bridget had her bed piled with twinkling lights, pink frilly bedding, and a gazillion pink sandals.

It was going to be a long, happy, pink year.

I sat on my bed and realized that I still held the unopened package from my mother. I squeezed the large envelope, wondering what it might be. The return address was somewhere in the UK. I tore the paper and tipped it over. A notebook, identical to the one my father had given me for my birthday, slid out. Bound with distressed leather, I opened it up and saw that he'd written on the first page:

To my darling daughter, Dakota. Record every moment, every thought, cherish your youth. Live the life you've always dreamed of. Love, Dad.

They were nice words, but words he should have said in person. Over the past few months, I'd seen him only once when he'd flown in and out for my graduation. Neither of my parents admitted to anything, but I could tell things weren't so good between them. They barely spoke two words to each other, and my dad left right after dinner. Said he had an important assignment that couldn't wait. As he left, he hugged me tightly and simply said he was sorry. For what? I didn't know. Maybe for everything. In any case, my list of father-daughter grievances was spectacularly long, so a simple "sorry" wasn't going to do the trick. Nevertheless, I couldn't help but worry. About him. My mother. Me. Our lives felt as though they teetered on the edge of a sharp knife, impending doom just around the corner.

That's really why this move felt more important than ever; I needed a fresh start. And to do that, I had to separate myself from their problems. It was the only way I would get my life back on track.

I glided my hand over the smooth leather of the notebook and then quickly dug out my favorite pen—it was a pink steel pen with little rhinestones that Mr. M had mailed to me as a graduation gift. He'd unexpectedly retired right after "the car incident," to follow his dream of becoming a writer. I hadn't seen him again, but I felt happy knowing he was somewhere out there, living his dream.

I slipped the pen into the special hidden slit in the binding of the notebook and read the inscription again. *Live the life you've always dreamed of.* That was exactly what I'd do.

I closed the notebook and held it to my chest. "Great idea." I sighed.

"What is? What's a great idea?" Bridget burst through the door, sweaty, skinny, panting. A tall and equally skinny brunet with glasses and wearing overalls stood beside her.

"Nothing," I replied. "Just talking to myself. I do that a lot. I'm sure you'll get used to it."

"Okay," she said cheerfully. "In case you get the urge to talk to real people, I'd like you to meet Christy, our next-door neighbor."

"Hi, I'm Dakota." I smiled and made a little wave.

"Hey. Nice to meet you," Christy said in quiet, little voice. Obviously, she was the shy type.

"Christy is a bio major—just like Lisa, Bren, and Taylor, who are also on the floor—crazy, huh?" How did Bridget know everyone already? Bridget snapped her fingers. "iPhone charger!" Bridget dug through one of her boxes and pulled out a tangled mess of cables. "Ah! Here it is." She handed it to Christy.

"You should come with us tonight," Bridget said to Christy, and I immediately wondered what she meant by "us." "There's a welcome cocktail at the Kappa House. And let me tell you, fifty of the hottest guys on campus will be there. Dakota's going." She looked at me. "Aren't you." It wasn't a question, but more of an affirmation.

I suddenly felt nervous. Downright panicky. My experience with guys hadn't been so positive.

Shut it, Dakota. This is what you're here for. You can do this.

"Absolutely," I replied. "You should come."

Christy made an awkward little chuckle and promised she'd go next time.

As soon as she left, Bridget looked at me. "Poor thing. We'll have to help her come out of that shell."

I was about to say how me helping anyone was ridiculous, but I squashed that little self-deprecating thought. "Sure. Just as soon as I'm done helping you."

She laughed. "If I became any more extraverted, I'd explode."

I could tell that Bridget was going to be a good influence.

"All right." She clapped her hands. "Time to get ready. Our destinies await!"

Oh God. I hope so.

۽ۙ

10:00 p.m. Kappa House

Though we'd scored a spot the next street over, parking was impossible. Cars piled up for ten blocks, with fifty more circling the neighborhood. And now, approaching the giant beach house, bursting with students, couples hooking up, and a multitude of dudes pounding beer on the enormous porch, I felt my pulse thump away at an unhealthy pace. "Are you sure we're invited?" I asked.

Bridget laughed. "Yeah, I'm sure."

I'd never been to a party-party, unless I counted the time Mandy's mother threw a champagne fund-raiser. I didn't drink, but I did get pretty wild with the karaoke.

"And we're not too late?" I asked.

"You're joking. Right? It's just getting started. My sister was a Tri Delta, and let me tell you, the parties she took me to last year never got going until midnight." I'd learned that Bridget grew up in L.A., but spent most weekends with her sister—a very recent UCSD grad—at the sorority house. Like me, Bridget had a working mother and absentee father, but a very cheery, pragmatic outlook on life.

I nodded. "Good to know."

Bridget stopped and leaned in, squinting in the dark. "Are you okay, Dakota? You look…kind of pale."

Welcome to Dakota-land. No tans. Only varying degrees of paleness. "I'm fine."

"Well, setting aside your terrified expression, you look hot. Hotter than hot. I'd give my right arm for that silky red hair. By the way, are those real? Not that I want to pry, but they're huge."

I glanced down at my chest. "Well, yeah. But they aren't that big."

She crinkled her brow. "Yeah. Whatever, Ms. Double D." She snorted. "Get it? Dakota Dane? DD?"

"Cute." I laughed politely, but what was all the fuss? They looked like normal Cs to me. Perhaps it was my strapless black blouse? A gift from Mandy. I hadn't really felt like unpacking yet, and it had been on the top of the pile inside my suitcase, as were my jeans. Add my favorite strappy, silver, platform sandals, and this was just about as good as it got in my fashion world. God, I missed Mandy already. Sadly, she was in New York enjoying the Manhattan life without me.

I followed Bridget up the crowded steps into the large, two-story house. It was what one might expect a well-financed frat house to look like: big wraparound porch, white. Other than the loud music and Greek shit hanging in the windows, it was picture-perfect.

I passed the threshold and gazed in wonder at the lively scene—laughter, dancing, drinking. It was exactly as I'd hoped my first college party would be, except…

My eyes immediately gravitated toward a familiar face in the crowd, and I instantly knew nothing would ever be right in my life again. Not for me. Not now. Not ever.

My dream of moving on would not be fulfilled.

"Santiago?"

CHAPTER FOURTEEN

Santiago stepped from the crowd wearing a navy-blue blazer, red tie, and tan pants, just like the other fraternity brothers who greeted guests—well, greeted girls mainly. With his messy, chin-length, almost-black hair, broad shoulders, and stubbled, angular jaw, I had to blink several times. Was he really there? This version looked older, more masculine, and more beautiful than before.

I stepped back, counter to the flow of the masses pouring inside.

"Don't be nervous," Bridget whispered, pulling my hand. "I know plenty of the sorority sisters who'll be here."

Santiago's feral gaze pierced through the crowd like a wolf that'd just spotted a juicy rabbit. I watched helplessly as he wove through the densely packed bodies.

This can't be happening. "Bridget, I left something in the car."

"It's not safe to walk alone…" Her voice trailed off as I bolted for my car.

I would call her later and pick her up. Or something. I didn't know. I just needed to get the hell out of there.

I glanced over my shoulder, but there wasn't anyone other than a few people walking into the party.

"Shit, shit, shit. This can't be happening." I got to my car, my hands trembling wildly as I dug for the keys in my purse. "Why me? Stupid Dakota. Stupid. You're going to ruin everything." *He can't be real. He can't be.*

Found 'em.

I slid inside the car, and my cell rang at the exact moment I started the engine. It was Bridget. "Hello?"

"Where did you run off to?" she asked.

"I…I…I'm not feeling well. I'm going back to the dorms to lie down. Call me when you're ready, okay? I'll come pick you up."

"Dakota." I jumped in my seat. Santiago's dark eyes studied me through a messy mop of dark hair. "Nice to see you again," he said in a menacingly low voice.

"Where did you come from?" I hadn't even heard the passenger door open.

He pushed back the seat to make room for his long legs and large frame. "You should listen to your roommate, it's not safe to walk alone at night."

I didn't know what to say. Was he real? Or had my mind decided that dreaming about him every single night was no longer enough. I dreamed of him standing guard outside my house, leaning on his gleaming chrome motorcycle, staring at my window while I watched him watching me. I dreamed of him kissing me, and of the heat of his body. I dreamed of him in my bed, blanketing me with his naked, hard muscles, and…

"Please tell me you're not real," I whispered.

He smiled in that arrogant kind of way. "Miss me that much, did you?"

Where had he gone? "Why are you back?"

He reached out and cupped my cheek, forcing me to look him straight in the eyes and triggering a flood of twisted, unwelcome emotions—fury, exhilaration, confusion. "Because you wanted me to come."

"No. No, I didn't." I could feel it, the hysterics building like a geyser about to explode. "I wanted to forget about you."

He tilted his gorgeous face to the side and studied me. His unshaved jaw worked a bit, before he parted those full lips and said, "I can see you're going to cause me problems again."

"Me? Cause *you* problems? Do you have any idea…"

Hell. I couldn't do this. I wasn't a scared little girl anymore. Whoever he was, whatever he was, he couldn't waltz into my life and ruin it. It was my life. "Get out. Get the fuck out of my car before I call the police."

Completely devoid of emotion, he bowed his head. "As you wish." He opened the passenger door and then paused. "You should know, however, that I'm not leaving you alone. So you can either make this easy or make this hard."

No, no, no. Not again. "What do you want?"

"To keep you safe. To make sure you live a long and happy life."

Safe? Long and happy life. Such bullshit! "Who are you?" I screamed.

The corner of his mouth turned up. "Have you forgotten the rule already? No questions." He slammed the door shut.

"You think you can come floating back into my life," I screamed at him as he stood there staring back through the window. Maybe he couldn't hear me, but it sure felt good. "But you can't. I have no idea who or what you are. But leave. Me. The. Fuck. Alone!"

He simply stared, a condescending look on his face.

Okay. This was ridiculous. This guy had to be some crazy stalker. I picked up my cell and dialed 911. I was going to report him. *Let the police figure out who he is!*

But when the phone rang, the dial tone changed from a ring to a beep and then disconnected.

I redialed and got the same result.

I stared at the phone, my mind completely boggled. I looked up, but Santiago wasn't there.

Okay. He'd done something to my phone with his psycho-stalker powers. Fine. But he couldn't stop me from going to the station.

I pulled out and headed toward the main avenue. Where the hell was the police station? I came to a red light and quickly searched on my phone. *Ha! Three blocks away!*

Within minutes, I was turning into the lot. I grabbed my purse and...

Holy shit.

There, standing in front of the station, leaning against a signpost that said Police Parking Only, stood Santiago. *Son of a bitch! He's a demon from hell!*

Well, he couldn't stop me from going in. I wouldn't let him control me. No, not again.

I marched straight for him, glaring with every step. Three steps from the door, a uniformed officer stepped out. The officer handed Santiago a large white envelope and shook his hand.

"Next time, don't wait so long to stop by," said the officer. "You know the door's always open."

My mouth hung open, and I stared with disgust. He had the SDPD in his pocket, too?

"Hey, John. I'd like you to meet Dakota Dane. The young lady I told you about."

The officer looked me over. "Is she all right? She looks a little pale?"

Santiago snickered under his breath. "She's a bit overwhelmed with the new campus, and it's her first time away from home."

"Well," said the officer to me, "just stick with Santiago here, he'll make sure you stay out of trouble." He slapped Santiago on the arm. "See you later."

I couldn't believe this.

I headed back to my car, refusing to turn around and look at those dark eyes. Likely he was smiling. Oh yes, with that mouth I wanted to punch.

I got into my red VW, put on my seat belt, and sucked in a breath. This couldn't be happening. It just…couldn't.

Back on the road, I ground my teeth and clenched the steering wheel so tightly that my palms burned. My rage had me completely unable to think straight. I wanted to kick that man. I wanted to jump on him and throttle his neck. I wanted him thrown in jail.

I thought about returning to the dorms, but I didn't want to hide in my room like a prisoner in my own life, so I headed back to the party.

A night like this called for shots.

ॐ

Confession time. I'd never had a drink before. Not a beer, glass of wine, or even a sip of a pink froufrou drink while my mother wasn't looking. That's why when Bridget handed me her red plastic cup, instructing me to wash the horrible tequila taste away, I chugged.

"Oh no, Dakota! I said wash it away, not down the entire cup." She reached into my jean pocket and snagged my keys. "Guess you won't be needing these."

"Why? I only had one shot. I'll be fine to drive in a few hours."

"Right. You have the look of someone who's just warming up."

Not really. Something that tasted so bad would have no way of making the situation better. Bottom line, either I was crazy or Santiago was some sort of super-stalker with mystical powers.

Worst of all, he was right. I *had* wished him back. I couldn't stop thinking about him, writing about him. His face. His body. His voice. Every night I dreamed of him, and no matter how angry I felt, no matter what my rational mind told me, the little part of my body that ruled my fantasies couldn't be shut off. Now, seeing him live produced some sort of Pavlovian response. I smelled him, my mouth watered. I saw him, my body tensed in places that had no business tensing. I heard his voice, pinpricks exploded over my skin.

Yes. I knew this wasn't normal in any way, shape, or form. I had found his picture online, claimed he was my boyfriend, and then he appeared in my life for a few days and promptly disappeared. Now he was back, and within seconds, my reality had turned into a hot, scrambled mess. Mentally and physically.

Judge me all you want, world, but there is no dancing around this. I am fucked. And no…"A tequila shot won't save me," I added to myself.

"You didn't have just one shot, you had six." Bridget laughed.

"Huh?" My mind bounced back to the here and now, but wasn't following.

"That cup you drank was pure tequila mixed with grenadine and a splash of pineapple."

Oh. So I'd just chugged down an entire semester's worth of shots. Great.

"Hey. Your cup is empty. Can I get you another?" A blond guy appeared at Bridget's side. He looked like an eager little puppy waiting for a treat.

"Let's dance," she said and grabbed his hand. "You don't mind, do you, Dakota?"

The blond guy looked at me. "You're not *the* Dakota, are you?"

What was he talking about?

My lack of response prompted him to say my last name.

"Do I know you?" I asked.

He chuckled. "No. But we all know *you*. By now every guy in school does." He wiggled his brows.

Oh great. I hadn't made it past the first day, and I was already the center of a sex scandal. For the record, I'd never even made it to first base. Pure as a boring patch of snow.

The blond guy patted me on the shoulder. "Oh. It's not that bad. I'm sure four years will go by quickly."

"Are you drunk? What are you talking about?" Bridget asked.

"Dakota here has made the blacklist. The first girl in, like, a decade."

"What?" I said.

"I think that's enough, Eric." Santiago appeared out of nowhere. "Why don't you take Bridget to dance."

Bridget's eyes lit up as she took Santiago in. "Sure," she looked at me, "I mean, if you're…"

"It's fine," I replied.

She walked away, gawking at Santiago's ass until she disappeared into the other room, where the music roared and bodies were dense.

"What did he mean 'blacklisted'?" I asked, fearful it was as bad as it sounded.

Santiago towered over me, but he suddenly looked like a kid who'd just been caught with his hand in the cookie jar.

"You weren't supposed to find out about that." He ran his hand through his dark hair.

"What did you do?" I seethed. "What is blacklisted?" I repeated.

Sensing imminent drama, a few people in the kitchen moved closer to listen. Santiago grabbed my hand and yanked me outside to the back porch where it was only slightly quieter, and occupied by couples kissing, enjoying the cool ocean breeze.

"I'm sorry, but it has to be this way."

"What way?" I asked.

"Like I said, you weren't supposed to know, but I suppose it's better you found out. Otherwise, you might think something's the matter with you."

No, no, no. I didn't like the sound of this at all. "What's going on?"

"Your name and picture have been circulated to every fraternity on campus. No one will go near you, at least, not in a nonacademic way."

He'd put the kibosh on anyone dating me?

"Well!" I threw up my hands. "At least you left me options in the non-Greek world."

He winced and then shook his head no.

He'd gotten the word out to the non-Greeks, too? But how? There were dozens of clubs, sports teams, and academic associations. It was impossible to get to every guy on campus. Wasn't it?

"How could you?" I fumed. And more importantly, I asked, "Why?"

"It's easier this way."

"Oh. I get it." The tequila kicked in, and my body felt surprisingly strong. I felt surprisingly courageous. I felt…angry! "You want to control me, own me. You sick…stalker!"

"My interest in you is purely…"

93

He was about to tip his hand. "What? Scientific? Professional? Extraterrestrial?"

He crossed his meaty arms over his chest.

"Okay. Well, I've had enough. You said you came back because I wished it. So now I wish you away. Shoo! Shoo!"

"Doesn't work like that. I'm not a genie—are you drunk?"

"Not yet, but as soon as the rest of that drink absorbs into my bloodstream, I sure the hell will be! And do you know what I'm going to do?"

The porch wobbled under my feet.

"Do tell, little girl."

Son of a—I slapped him hard. "Don't you dare talk to me like that. You...*monster*."

I stomped inside and charged through the kitchen into the overcrowded living room where I found Bridget dancing with that blond guy. I threw my arms into the air and let out a "Woo!" that was echoed by the rowdy crowd. The tequila made a warm home inside my chest and urged me to do many things I'd regret in the morning. *Like kissing that really hot guy with the big blue eyes who's watching you dance?*

I beckoned him with my index finger, surprised when it actually worked. He was even cuter up close.

"Hi. What's your name?" he asked, rubbing himself against me to the beat of the music—it was impossible not to, given how crowded the room was.

"I'm...*Jane*!" Dakota was, after all, blacklisted. But not Jane.

"Mike."

"Hi, Mike. I hope you don't mind, but I really want to kiss you."

Yep. That was the tequila speaking.

"Okay by me." He dipped his head and pressed his lips to mine. I wrapped my arms around his neck and let 'er rip. But instead of seeing Mike, I only saw my sexy ghost.

God, it felt so wrong. So sinful. But I knew it wasn't the real thing, and that just made it even better. It was only safe when Santiago remained in the confines of fantasyland. I leaned into Mike and savored the feeling of his hands running over my body.

I expected at any moment to feel Santiago's real hands prying us apart. But that didn't happen. When I broke the kiss and looked up, I merely saw Santiago leering from across the room. He lifted his beer in my direction as if to say, "Enjoy the day."

I nodded at him. *I intend to.*

Then he disappeared.

Bastard.

Surprisingly, the rest of the evening did not turn into that cliché of a college freshman girl away from home for the first time with access to unlimited alcohol. In fact, I felt quite proud. I kissed. I danced. I drank an incredible amount of water. I did not vomit on anyone's hydrangeas or pass out. I didn't end up in some strange guy's bed. Nope. I walked out of the party with my chin held high, a giant blister on my toe, and a sober chauffeur, Bridget, to take us home.

As Mike and that blond guy from earlier—Eric—walked us to my car, I kept flashing glances over my shoulder, expecting Santiago to jump out from the bushes and beat the crap out of them. Or bark orders at me. Or throw me over his shoulder like his prized kill. No, I hadn't seen him for hours, but I still felt his eyes on me, watching from somewhere. Or maybe it was simply a really bad case of paranoia. A completely justified case of paranoia!

Bridget and Eric talked and giggled quietly before she loaded herself into the driver's seat. Mike was about to kiss me when Eric said, "Dude. No. Don't kiss her."

Mike looked at him as if he were asking for an ass whooping.

"Dude," Eric said, "that's Dakota Dane."'

Mike looked down at me. "But you said your name was Jane."

"I—I don't know what this blacklisting crap is, but it doesn't involve me."

Mike stepped back. "Are you trying to ruin my life?"

"No—I…"

He walked away. No, wait. He ran away. As quickly as his feet could carry him.

I slid into the passenger side of my car and closed the door. *Damn it!* Was this why Santiago didn't jump all over the guy? He knew this would happen!

"Well," Bridget said, "that blacklist thing is certainly going to put a huge crimp in your social life. Once you're on, it's almost impossible to be removed. So, who'd you piss off?"

I shrugged. "I wish I knew."

CHAPTER FIFTEEN

The next morning, like so many mornings before this one, I rolled over in bed, half-awake, thinking that the events of the prior day had been a dream. Nothing but a bad, bad dream. But as my mind floated up from the depths of a sleepy swamp, I knew in my gut that Santiago's return was real. And while a tiny part of me couldn't help but feel fascinated—the man was a walking, talking question mark with killer looks—my saner side knew better.

Question was, what was I going to do about him? What *could* I do about him? Tell the police, the FBI? File a restraining order? Laws couldn't stop a man who seemed to know my every move, who knew my secrets, who had connections with everyone. No solution fit, but I wasn't about to give up. And I'd be damned if I would let him take away my dreams.

I quickly dialed my father and got his voicemail. I left an urgent message and then tried my mother.

Voicemail. Damn it!

All right. Breathe. Calm yourself. Think. I pondered for several moments, but came up empty-handed in the solutions department. As for emotions? I had an abundance of those; primarily pissed off. Santiago's unexpected return would not deter me from my mission—having a life! A perfect life. Which is exactly what I planned to do while I figured this out.

Wanting to let Bridget sleep, I grabbed my clothes, showered, dressed, and went to the café to pick up a much-needed coffee before heading off to buy books and explore the campus.

Maybe I'd call Bridget later to check out the beach or do a little shopping downtown.

But as I strolled the manicured grounds between modern buildings of steel and glass, map in one hand, coffee in the other, I found myself looking over my shoulder and feeling the need to check out every student, just to be sure they weren't Santiago in disguise or something. I couldn't shake the feeling of his eyes on me.

My phone vibrated in my pocket, and I groaned. My hands were full, so I walked over to a bench and set down my cup so I could dig for the phone.

I looked at the screen. *Santiago. How did I know?* I answered but didn't say anything.

"Good morning. How's your coffee?"

Shit. I spun around but saw only backpack-toting students, trees, and buildings. *Son of a bitch.*

I didn't reply.

"The silent treatment again, I see," he said.

That's right, you psycho.

"So, you're still upset then?" he asked.

Yep. You got it!

"I don't blame you. That's why I wanted you to know that it wasn't supposed to be like this again."

"Like what? You mysteriously showing up like a creepy stalker on my first day of college, ruining my life with your sick mind games, and destroying any chance I have of getting a date?"

There was an awkward silence before he responded. "Your father is coming soon. Yes?"

What the hell kind of answer was that? "Yes. Why?"

"Be ready."

The call dropped and my blood pressure dropped right with it. I immediately dialed my father again, but it went to voicemail as expected. I hesitated for a moment, tempted to leave a scathing message, but hung up and dialed my mother again instead. The call also went straight to voicemail. "Mom. It's me. We need to talk. Santiago is back. He's saying I should 'be ready' for Dad's visit. Do you know what's going on?" I sighed loudly. "Call me, okay?"

I headed toward the bookstore, fuming. I was not going to let this happen. This was my life. Whatever weirdness was going on, whatever that "be ready" crap meant, I was not going to curl into a little ball and cower.

"You are not ruining my day!" I barked to an imaginary Santiago. Or maybe not. Maybe he could hear me.

I threw my coffee in the trash, got out my class syllabi, and marched into the crowded store.

It took me twenty minutes to cool off and find my way around, and another forty to find my books. Distracted and mumbling angrily under my breath, I went to the back of the line, which snaked around the entire edge of the store, and plunked my basket onto the floor. *He's not getting away with this. I don't care if that bastard owns my dreams; he can't have the daytime, too.*

"I'm taking that class, too."

I looked up and saw a tall, blond guy wearing shorts and a T-shirt, staring down at my chemistry book. He had a boyish smile and blue eyes. Pretty cute, actually.

I suddenly felt completely embarrassed. Had he heard me spouting off to myself?

I cleared my throat. "Professor Robins? Tuesday and Thursday at 2:00 p.m?" I said.

"Yep. Me, too," he said happily. "I hear she's tough, especially on her undergrads—feels it's her mission to toughen everyone up for upper-division courses."

"Oh. I hadn't heard that. But I know there's a chemistry club. I'm thinking of joining," I said.

He raised his brows. Had I sounded too geeky? This was college. Wasn't being academic cool now?

"Well, if I have time for it," I added. "So much fun stuff going on around here. Beach, parties, yunno." *Why did I say that? Woman up, Dakota.* "But I'm signing up for chem club right after this."

His smile returned. "Cool. Well, if you want a study partner, let me know. I'm Greg, by the way." He held out his hand.

"Dakota Dane." I shook his hand and watched the color drain from his face. "What's the matter?"

"Oh. Shit. Yunno, I forgot my wallet in the dorm. Guess I'll have to come back later." He set his pile of books on a shelf.

"I can hold your place," I said. "I'm sure it'll be an hour before we get to the register."

"Uh. No. No, thanks. I don't mind coming back later. It's no big deal."

"Okay. See you in class?" I said, but he was already halfway out the door.

I sighed. "Blacklisted." This wasn't happening.

૭✈◌

The next day, I went to a freshman safety orientation, met Bridget's sorority sisters-to-be, and attended a welcome party at the beach. I wish I could say I was enjoying the incredible experience of college life and meeting new people, but each time I had to introduce myself to anyone, especially guys, I found myself shrinking away or making some lame excuse to leave. What if they recognized my name?

It completely sucked.

When classes finally started on Wednesday, I felt a sense of relief. I could focus on something other than my nonexistent social life. That relief evaporated, though, the moment I sat down in the front row, ready to take my very first college course, when my advanced calculus professor called my name. A low murmur broke out in the room behind me, and the guy next to me, some straggly haired stoner-looking guy, got up and moved.

What the hell? This felt all too reminiscent of being the plague of humanity in high school, except that I didn't have Mandy.

How dare Santiago! How dare he do this to me! I sat up straight and channeled my rage into extremely thorough note taking. The moment the professor ended his lecture, I was out the door and calling Santiago. Unlike any of the other times I'd called his number, this time it rang. He immediately picked up, but didn't say anything.

"I know you're listening, you fucking bastard. I'm not going to let you do this. I'm not letting you take away my life."

"What if I'm helping you keep it?" he said in a low, no-nonsense tone.

"Bullshit!" I barked, storming through campus. It was a bright sunny morning, and the campus crawled with students who now veered from my path, afraid I'd gone postal. "You listen to me, Santiago. You will take my name off that blacklist. You will never come near me again. If you do, so help me God, I will rip out your heart."

I heard a faint chuckle on the other end of the phone.

"What?" I seethed. "You think this is funny!"

"Not at all," he replied. "I was thinking that you actually look like you might tear out my heart. It's a relief to see you stand up for yourself like this."

"A relief?" I stopped and swiveled on my heel. "Where are you?" I knew he was watching me.

"You just told me that you don't want to see me."

"I changed my mind," I growled.

A long pause. "Maybe the blacklist was a bit overprotective. I'll see what I can do to have it lifted," he said.

That was great, but we still had an issue.

"Not good enough. I want you out of my life. Gone," I said. "I mean it."

"I can't do that," he replied coldly.

"Then expect a fight."

I ended the call and tried my dad again. *Voicemail. Shit.* I called my mother and got hers, too.

What's with these two? Maybe my dad was out of cell range—it happened when he went on shoots out in the boonies—but my mother usually called right back. Especially when I left an urgent message as I had done multiple times over the past few days.

I dialed my Aunt Rhonda, who immediately answered. But when I asked her if she'd heard from my mom, she told me not to worry. "She probably forgot to charge her phone again and hasn't noticed. Why? Is something wrong, honey?" she asked.

What could I tell her that wouldn't sound insane? "No— uhhh. Can you tell her I need to talk to her, though, if you hear from her?"

"Sure, Dakota. But are you certain everything's okay? How are you liking college?"

"Yeah. You know. It's college. I just need to talk to her about books and a couple of things. But, ummm, I need to run to class. I'll call you later and tell you all about it. Okay?"

I hung up, scratching my head. My mother never forgot to charge her phone. Something wasn't right, and an uneasy feeling washed over me.

CHAPTER SIXTEEN

I didn't see or hear from Santiago for the next few days, but I knew he was there, watching. Even more annoying was that my dreams were completely contaminated by him. Sometimes they were dreams of him hunting me, but usually they were explicit dreams of us doing very explicit things: ravaging each other on the beach in broad daylight; making slow, passionate love next to a campfire—he loved camping, after all—and, of course, the shower.

It seemed that my immature hormones had followed me to college.

But I wasn't going to let him win. I would find a way to extract him from my life. In fact, I'd already decided to go to the FBI on Monday. The only thing that made me uneasy was that part about him telling me to get prepared for my dad.

On the bright side, my mother *finally* texted me and said that she was at some spa retreat up in Napa with her girlfriends. I guess with me out of the house, she could finally take time for herself, which was awesome. Although, I still couldn't shake that feeling of something not being right, like she was avoiding me. When I texted her back about Santiago showing up, and me needing to talk to her and Dad, she replied she'd try to track Dad down and call me later. That was all. Strange, to say the least. Almost as strange as the last time I'd mentioned Santiago and she did that weird thing with her face, and then pretended I hadn't said anything. Maybe she really was afraid I'd gone bonkers.

In any case, I'd survived my first week of college and held myself together despite the bizarre noise in the background of my life. Of course, that's because I'd kept myself insanely distracted—joined a few study groups, went to my first chem club, signed up to volunteer for the beach cleanup crew with our neighbor Christy, and Skyped with Mandy two nights in a row. I couldn't believe the transformation. Her personality, her enthusiasm, even her clothes. She'd become a metropolitan socialite overnight. She said New York was hands down *the* most exciting place in the world, and made me promise to visit for the weekend. Given how expensive tickets were, I'd probably see her back home for Christmas before I'd get out there.

So while Mandy was out exploring the city nightlife with her new fashion friends, I planned to snack my way through Friday night and have a little History Channel alien documentary marathon on my laptop, after I had a quick therapy session.

I pulled out my brand-new journal, the one my father had given me, and looked at its exquisite workmanship. The leather binding, the thick paper, the embossing with my name. I'd have to ask him where he bought these because I'd never go back to a cheesy drugstore journal. I got out my favorite pen and started writing down the events of my first few days of college. I left everything out about Santiago. He wasn't welcome in my memories. He was a ghost, I determined, and ghosts belonged in the shadows, confined to the realm of whispers and folklore.

"You coming?" Bridget popped her head inside the room. She wore a low-cut, baby-blue tank and her infamous short shorts. I wished I could get away with that outfit, but the Dane women were built for endurance and plowing fields or lifting cranes, or some shit like that. There wasn't anything wrong with my body, but it simply wasn't short shorts material.

"I think I'm going to stay in tonight. Get caught up on my shows."

Bridget hissed. "Let me get this straight. It's your first Friday away from home, possibly the biggest party night of the year, given it's also pledge week, and you want to stay in our icky, gray dorm room? Get the hell out! You can watch TV tomorrow while you're nursing a hangover."

"No. I'm really—"

"You owe me a chauffeur."

I looked at her and narrowed my eyes. "Not fair. Wait. I thought you said I'd be nursing a hangover?"

"Did I say that?" she replied with a guilty grin. "I meant you can watch TV tomorrow while *I'm* nursing a hangover. 'Cause you're driving."

I rolled my eyes. I didn't want to go out. Not when I might bump into Santiago.

"Come on. Eric is going to be there, and I really want to see him again."

"You're going to Kappa House again?" I asked.

"Yeah. It'll be fun! Come on," she whined.

You promised yourself you weren't going to let him win. You can't stay hidden in your room.

I gave it a few moments of thought. *Actually, going isn't such a bad idea.* Maybe I could get one of the Kappas to dish something about Santiago. Where he came from. Who he was. Why they all seemed to know him. I could also check to see if he'd lifted the Dakota ban.

You're lying to yourself, and you know it. You want to see him. Maybe a part of me did, but a stronger part of me wanted to go there to satisfy my urge to show him that I wasn't afraid.

"Okay," I said, "I'll drive. But can we come back early? I don't want to be burned out tomorrow. Lots of studying to do."

Bridget rolled her eyes. "Ugh. Okay. But wear something mildly presentable, okay? Our Delta sisters will be there. By the way, Kelly Flores, the president of the sorority, asked about you today."

"She did? What did she want to know?" I asked.

Bridget crinkled her face into that ugly ball. "Actually, she asked about that guy you were talking to at the party on Monday. She wanted to know if you and he were dating."

"Why would she want to know that?" I asked.

Bridget made a little shrug. "Um, because he's quite possibly the hottest man on the planet? So are you seeing him?" she asked.

"No, definitely not."

"That's what I told Kelly. I mean, you did make out with that Mike guy right in front of him."

"Then why does she think we're dating?" I asked.

"I don't know. Kelly mentioned that she bumped into him at the café yesterday, and he'd talked about you for ten minutes. Like he was in love with you. But then when she asked if you two were together, he made a weird comment—like, 'hell would sooner freeze over.'"

I admit I felt a tiny blister appear on my ego. "Nope. Not seeing him. Nor do I ever intend to."

Bridget released a breath. "Good. Because I think Kelly wants to ask him out or something. Wouldn't want anything to get in the way of you joining the Tris."

I hadn't actually decided I wanted to pledge a sorority, but Bridget seemed to have her heart set on us joining together, and I didn't want to tell her no. She would never understand the turmoil lurking just below the surface of my life, like a bad rash waiting to erupt.

"I'll be ready in ten," I said.

"Yippy!" She clapped. "And don't forget to put on something smashing, *darrrling*!"

"But of course, *darrrling*." I grabbed my makeup bag and headed for the bathroom. Maybe she was right, I should get dressed up. If Santiago had lifted the ban, then I was fair game now. Nothing like a pretty dress to get the guys talking to you.

I just hoped he'd kept his word. Otherwise, there'd be no talking, only screaming. With my knee. In his groin.

శ్రీ

At eleven o'clock, Bridget and I arrived at Kappa House. Unlike Monday night, which was fun and only slightly wild, tonight was *Animal House* on steroids. It was a complete shock that the police weren't camped outside issuing noise citations or throwing everyone in jail for public drunkenness. "How are all these people getting home?" I asked.

Bridget pointed to a guy wearing a red tie. Yes, T-shirt, shorts, flip-flops, and a red tie. "He's a pledge. Pledges never drink. They only get to drive people around."

Oh. Made sense.

I turned to say something to Bridget, but she disappeared instantly, leaving me standing by myself in a loud ocean of students, smushed together, dancing, talking, trying not to spill their plastic cups filled with beer. I sighed and decided to work my way to the kitchen. Maybe I'd find that Mike guy or maybe I'd—

"Miss Dane. It's nice to see you, as always."

Santiago had popped out of nowhere, and the moment I turned, his eyes dropped to my chest. Yes, my tight, red, fitted dress was the lowest cut thing I owned. And honestly, I looked pretty good. Santiago's sweeping eyes confirmed it.

And—kick me hard—but he looked incredible. He wore a fitted, white linen shirt that accentuated his broad shoulders and lean, well-built physique—sleeves rolled up to expose his hard, tanned forearms—and soft, worn jeans that embraced every manly angle of his manly lower half.

"Great," I said dryly. "My ghost is back. You're actually becoming pretty predictable." Even in my dreams he was predictable. He always started out by laying me down on my back and then allowing me to watch him remove his shirt, his thick biceps flexing as he worked his buttons to expose the chiseled mounds of his deeply tanned pectorals—

Santiago snapped his fingers in my face. "Dakota?"

I looked up at him and swallowed. "Yeah?" The word came out all scratchy.

"I asked you a question," he said.

"Yeah?" I said. I could barely remember where I was.

"Why are you here?" he asked.

"Why are *you* here?" I asked.

"I'm here because you're here."

"Oh. To make sure I'm 'safe and happy'?" I used my fingers to make air quotes.

"That's exactly right."

"I'm here to find a way to get rid of you," I said.

He smiled, flashing a tiny little dimple in his right cheek. "Is that right?"

"That's right."

"You know that will never happen." His tone was playful and borderline smug. Why didn't he take any of this seriously?

"Do you have any idea how old this is getting, this…enigma, mystery man crap?"

"I'm sure it is. But it's better than the alternative."

"Which is?" I asked.

Goofing around, two large dudes shuffled past and bumped me right into Santiago's arms. My chest smashed against his body, our faces so close I could smell his sweet breath—cinnamon mixed with something kind of minty.

Eyes locked, the two of us just stood there as people passed by laughing, screaming, and singing. I couldn't help it, but him holding me so tightly, our hips pressed together, our lips within an easy distance, created tiny explosions of pinpricks throughout my body.

He stared into my eyes for what seemed like an eternity and then his gaze slowly slid to my lips. Kick me again, but I realized that I wanted him to kiss me. I wanted it so badly that I started to lean in just as he did.

Wait. What's wrong with me? I can't be trusted around him. He's like kryptonite for intelligence!

I quickly pushed back. "All right. You win, Santiago. I'm done." Coming to the party had been a stupid idea.

"Where are you going?"

"To find Bridget. Maybe one of the pledges can drive her home." I couldn't take this anymore. The strangeness of the situation was simply too much, and though I'd tried to be strong and believe there were reasons for all this, I wouldn't lie to myself anymore. The entire thing was terrifying. I had no control over my emotions when I was around him. This situation felt like being right back in high school, reliving those final months spinning in my head instead of enjoying life. After Janice was gone, I had a ton of offers for the senior ball. Boys actually wanted to date me, and the other girls were nice to me. I'd finally ditched my Queen Loser title, but instead of enjoying it, I spent every day wondering if Santiago might return. I woke up nightly in a cold sweat for months until I finally made a deal with myself. I'd promised that the moment I graduated and moved off to college, the past would stay behind.

"Dakota, don't leave." Santiago grabbed my hand.

I yanked it away. "Don't. Don't touch me." I pushed my way to the front door, nearly stumbling in my red heels as I hit the stairs. The tears begged me to let them loose, but there was no way I'd let this man see my cry.

"Dakota," Santiago ran ahead and blocked me with his body. Once again I found our bodies pressed together. I looked up at him, unable to speak. Feeling his warmth and his arms gripping me tightly triggered that damned Pavlovian response. I didn't think. I just…was.

He brought his hand to my cheek and whisked away a tear that had escaped. "I'm sorry. But it has to be this way."

"You've ruined my life," I whispered. "I'm crazy."

"You're not crazy."

"Really? Really? Because I'm pretty damned sure I am. For fuck's sake, I found your picture on the Internet. I made you up! Then there you were! And then you disappeared. So please, please try to explain in which universe the definition of crazy doesn't fit?"

I attempted to wriggle away, but he pulled me closer.

His eyes drilled me with his intense emotions. "I know this is hard. But you're alive. And I'll be damned if I fail to keep you that way because you can't handle a few ambiguities."

Was that what he thought this was about? Ambiguities? How could he think that when he'd just said he was keeping me alive? So who wanted to hurt me and why? But, of course, he wasn't going to tell me anything. That much I knew.

I studied his face, trying to put the pieces together. Nothing fit. Nothing. Especially the fact that when I was near him, I felt safe. And now, pressed firmly against his strong body, I couldn't stop my body from reacting.

"I'm going home," I said.

"You're upset. I'll take you."

"Leave me alone, Santiago." I tried to shake him off me, but it only made him madder.

He raised his voice, "I can't do that, Dakota."

"Your fucking problem! Let me go!" I jerked away and ran to my car, heading straight for the dorms the moment I started the engine.

Damn it! Santiago was behind me on his motorcycle. *Son of a bitch.*

A few minutes later, I arrived at the parking lot. It was crowded with fire trucks and police cars everywhere. I pulled into a spot and got out of the car. Smoke poured from one of the windows on the top floor.

I scrambled over to a group of girls standing near the mob of spectators, half of them wearing pajamas. "What happened?" I asked.

"Someone started a fire," one of them responded. I recognized her as being from my floor. "That girl over there said she saw a guy running down the hall right when the flames burst out." She pointed to a brunet talking to the police. I looked up again and noticed the stream of water from the hoses pointed at the room next to mine.

"They're saying that poor girl Christy was inside."

What? "Christy? You mean glasses-wearing, bio-major Christy?"

The girl nodded and my heart skipped a beat. "Are you sure?" There had to be a mistake.

"The firefighters already carried her away in an ambulance. They had her face covered, but it had to be her. Her roommate is gone for the weekend."

Oh my God. "Christy's dead?" I felt like the wind had been knocked out of me.

"Dakota?" I heard Santiago's deep voice behind me.

"Get away from me." I marched back to my car, determined to find somewhere else to have my breakdown.

Santiago caught up before I managed to open the door. "Damn it, Dakota. Stop. Just…stop."

"What?" I stomped. "What do you want from me? To see me crumble? To see me fall into the world's tiniest pieces, so small that no one can ever find me? Because that's where I'm heading!" I pounded his hard chest. "I'm not like you! I'm a person. I'm real, Godfuckingdamn it!"

It's not that I knew Christy well, but I'd already reached my limit. This was the final mental straw. *That poor girl. Her poor family.*

He pulled me into him, cupping my head to his chest. "I know," he whispered, stroking the back of my head. The tears broke free. "I know," he repeated, but his words didn't make me feel any better. His strength and warmth did, however. They made me feel safe enough to let go. So that's what I did, knowing how wrong it was to find comfort in him.

Several minutes passed, but then Santiago's body became rigid. "You can't stay here." Santiago's firm grip led me toward the passenger side of my car.

"Where are you taking me?" I said between tiny sobs as I slid into the car. The shock had my brain all twisted in knots.

Santiago came around and got into the driver's seat. "You can stay with me tonight."

What? Christ. "No way."

"Where else are you going to go?" His phone rang, and he dug it out of his pocket. "Yeah?" He listened for several moments. "That's good, I guess. But we need to talk." Pause. "Fine. But I'm not doing this anymore." Another pause. "You made a promise. So either keep it, or I'm done." He scratched his forehead. "All right. You know where to find me."

"Who was that?" I asked.

Santiago cranked the engine. "The man who's going to give you answers."

I wiped the tears from my eyes. *The man? What man?* "What do you mean?"

"Exactly what I said."

"Why can't you tell me?" Because, if he hadn't noticed, I was snapping.

"'Cause it'll be my ass." He paused, his jaw flexing. "But if he doesn't tell you the truth, then I will."

"When?" I asked. "Tonight?" He couldn't drop a bomb like that at a time like this and expect me to just remain calm. There was someone behind all this crap.

He released a slow breath. "No. But soon. And trust me, you don't want to know tonight. You've been through enough already."

The word "soon" jogged my memory. Santiago had asked me about my father coming "soon" and then had said to get ready. "Wait. Does this have something to do with my dad?"

Santiago ran his hand over the steering wheel and then gave me a sharp look. "Do you trust me?"

I did and I didn't. I trusted he would do anything to keep me out of harm's way, including hurt me if need be. It was seriously complicated.

I shrugged.

"Fair enough. All I'm asking is for a few more days. I promise you'll get every answer coming to you. Even the ones I know you'll wish you hadn't heard."

PART THREE

One Hundred Percent

Chance

of Rabbit Holes

CHAPTER SEVENTEEN

By the time we arrived at his small beach house, I could barely breathe or move; the shock was taking its toll. Not only because of all that was happening to me, but because that sweet girl had died. I couldn't stop thinking about how insanely precious life was.

But I already knew that. I'd known it from the moment I was five and my mother came home from work, blood covering the front of her scrubs. She hadn't known I was there watching and listening from the hallway, but what she told my Aunt Rhonda would probably stay with me until the day I died: "He was just a baby," she'd sobbed. "Just a baby no older than Dakota. What's the point of being born if some asshole can just take it away in the blink of an eye?"

I never found out what happened to that little boy, but many weeks later, I remember asking my mother what she thought "the point" was. Why *were* we here? I recalled her warm blue eyes as she smiled and brushed her hand over the top of my head. "To live. And if we're lucky, to love."

From then on, "living" felt like a sacred mission, an unattainable state of perfection, some obscure mountain I would someday climb if I were good enough. It became a mild obsession. I constantly thought about what my future would be like when I started "to live." *I* wanted to be one of those perfect people in the TV commercials who laughed and ran on the beach, holding hands with someone she loved, who was equally perfect. Silently sitting with Santiago in the car, I realized that was my hang-up. The source of all my dysfunction. That picture-perfect life and picture-perfect person I'd dreamt of being didn't exist, nor would she ever. Yet I chastised myself for every flaw, every mistake. I called myself a loser. Queen Loser. The older I got, and the more I grew to know myself, the more I realized how imperfect I was. And the more imperfect I was, and the farther I got from my goal of "living" that perfect life, the more I hated myself.

What an idiot.

I'd spent so much time thinking about the future and about becoming someone I could never be that I'd simply missed the point: I was alive. Now. This very moment. And that's all there was. It could be messy and horrible and consist of the most improbable circumstances, but that was all any of us truly had. One blink, and it could all be gone. Just like Christy.

So what should I do?

Brace yourself. Whatever answers were coming, and whoever would be giving the answers, I knew they were going to bulldoze over a lifetime of sandcastles. And I had to decide right then and there whether I'd let it ruin me.

Santiago turned off the engine. "We're here."

He led me inside and flipped on a lonely lamp in the entryway. "I'm renting this place," he said quietly. "But you're safe here."

I nodded. *Safe. Safe. Safe...*What did that mean? Did I want safe anymore? Wasn't it just another illusion?

He walked me down a long, dark hall into a bedroom. I was too fried to notice anything other than Santiago and the bed.

"Sit," he said.

I did, and he left for a moment and returned with a tall glass of water.

"Drink," he instructed.

I once again obeyed.

"You okay?" he asked.

I nodded, staring at the floor.

"Why don't you lie down? Try to get some sleep."

I looked up at his beautifully masculine face. "Don't leave. Okay?"

The corner of his mouth twisted a bit, as if he was uncomfortable with my request. Then he smiled. "Okay. But keep your hands off my ass."

I flopped back into the bed, exploding with laughter until my cheeks hurt. When my chuckle died, I glanced at Santiago, standing to my side, arms crossed, smiling. "I like your laugh. You should do it more often."

I sighed. "Thanks."

We stared at each other for a moment before he jarred himself from my gaze. "I'll go make you a sandwich. I hope you like grilled cheese."

"Love grilled cheese."

"Be back in a few. Stay put." He disappeared down the hall, and I sat staring at the ceiling, thinking about all of the pieces I'd been trying to force-fit into my perfect little puzzle.

It was time to let it all go. Whatever was coming, it sure as hell wouldn't be perfect, and now it was up to me to find a way to live. Come what may.

෯෯

I didn't know the time, but it was still dark out when I woke up to Santiago's mumbling, his arms wrapped around my waist, his face nuzzled in my hair. An uneaten sandwich sat on the nightstand by my head, and the lamp had been left on.

"You're safe. I promise," he whispered. "Just don't give up."

Was he dreaming?

"Why did you say that?" I asked.

"I'll probably die for you, and it has to mean something."

What? I turned my head and looked at him. He was sound asleep.

Who knows what he was dreaming about, but I couldn't help noticing how lying in his arms made me feel safe. Tormented. Safe. Insane. Alive.

I closed my eyes and drifted back to sleep.

CHAPTER EIGHTEEN

"Ummm…Santiago," I groaned.

He'd removed his shirt, jeans, and hovered over my body. His feral, dark eyes drilled into me. "Are you sure, Dakota?"

I nodded, biting my lips.

He gripped my panties and tugged them down, gazing hungrily at the valley between my legs. "Have you…?"

Did he mean been with someone? As in was I a virgin?

I slowly shook my head. "No. I've never…"

He tilted his head, and his dark hair fell to one side. "Then I'll take it slow."

He slid down his boxers and allowed me to take in the impressive view. The thickness was not what I'd expected. Neither was its length. He was much larger.

He flashed that charming, arrogant smile and lay over me.

"Don't move an inch," he said. He rubbed the silky soft head of his penis against my throbbing bud.

"Dakota?"

"Umm…Yeah?"

"Open your eyes. Look at me."

I did as he asked.

"You were dreaming, weren't you?"

I took a moment to digest.

Santiago and I were facing each other, fully clothed, my legs woven between his, his between mine.

My eyes scanned the room. It was furnished with simple, sleek modern furniture, white walls, a large walk-in closet.

"Where are we?" I whispered.

"My place. And if you don't take your hand off me, I won't be responsible for my actions."

Hmmm… Yes. In fact, my hand was gripping a very large, hard, and warm object.

Horrified, I quickly let go. "I am so, so sorry—"

"Not as sorry as I am." He grinned.

"Get the fuck away from my daughter."

I looked up. "Daddy?"

ॐॐ

Yeah. If I could pick the top three situations a girl could live without, having your father catch you in bed with a guy while gripping his raging hard-on would be number one. Not sure what number two or three would be, but who cared? They were distant runners-up.

"I said, get the fuck off her." My dad's steel-gray eyes glowed with fury.

Santiago, calmly and slowly, slid from the blankets holding up his palms as if he were a 7-Eleven clerk being held up at 3:00 a.m., with no hope of survival.

"Dakota, go back to your dorm," my father said. With his cropped silver hair slightly disheveled and his dark gray designer suit excessively wrinkled, I knew he'd just gotten off a plane. From where? Who knew.

"What are you doing here?" I asked.

My father gave me a look that could send a person straight to hell. "Dorm!" he barked.

"But my room is—"

"Fine!" His face turned bright red. "Your room is fine. The fire damage is next door."

"But why are you he—"

"Go," Santiago growled. "Your father and I need to talk in private."

I knew better than to argue with my father, but what the hell was Santiago thinking? My father was a large man, almost as tall as Santiago, and certainly as intimidating.

I got up from the bed, thankful to see my nudity had only been a dream, but unthankful to leave my ghost behind with a man who looked like he might make him a ghost for real.

I glanced back at Santiago, who gave me a nod. "It's fine."

Yeah. But he didn't know my father. Dad hadn't built his thriving company on kindness or warm fuzzies.

"Wait." The fog of sleep lifted from my head, and my thoughts skidded to a stop. "You two know each other?"

My father glared at me. "Yes. And I'll explain everything later."

Oh hell no! "So it *is* you? You're behind all this? You're this…*man* with the answers?"

I glanced at Santiago, but his ice-cold gaze gave nothing away.

My father grumbled under his breath. "Dakota, honey. I promise everything will make sense."

"But I—"

My father held up his hand. "Go to the dorms, pack your things. I'll be right behind you."

"You're taking me home?" I asked, unsure if this was a good or bad thing. Home sounded kind of nice right about now.

"I'm taking you to an apartment off campus."

I guessed he wanted to do that because of the fire, but I wasn't going anywhere. "Hold on—"

"Now!" he screamed.

I stared for several moments, thinking through the options. There was no use in talking to the man when he was pissed. Anyone who'd spent more than five seconds with him knew that much. But did he honestly believe that a little bullying would frighten me away? After everything I'd been through?

"I'll wait outside. You're coming with me to the dorms, right?" I said to Santiago.

My father looked at me. "Santiago won't be joining us." His gaze bounced back to Santiago. "Will you?"

What the hell was going on? I looked at Santiago, then at my father, and then back again.

Santiago's expression was as cool and deadly as a morgue freezer. "Guess not," he said to my father.

"Best say your good-byes now," my father said to me.

Good-bye? Good-bye?

I looked at Santiago once again, but he ignored me, and it stung. I wasn't really sure why, but it did.

Suddenly, I didn't care what was happening or what my father had to do with this mess; I simply wanted to leave and not have to look at either of them.

"You both disgust me," I seethed. "And don't bother coming to my dorm. I don't want to see either of you again."

Furious, I left the house, got in my car, and drove down the coast back to campus, my mind unable to form a coherent thought. *My father and Santiago know each other. My father is in San Diego. He knew I was at Santiago's house. My father is behind everything! Why would he put me through all this? And is Santiago really gone from my life?* My mind whirled and spun and made random loop-the-loops, but nothing connected.

How could my father know some random guy I found on the Inter—

Shit, shit, shit. The photo wasn't random.

I gasped.

When I'd opened my laptop on that fateful day of deceit to create my fake boyfriend, my browser had been parked on my father's website. Being a photographer, he had tons of links leading to portfolios, advertising various shoots he'd done over the years.

Christ. That's it. I'd followed one of the links.

How could I have not remembered that? The link had a gorgeous photo of a man standing on the beach, looking out across the waves. I remember being captivated by that tormented look in his eyes, and thinking how I felt just like him.

So…Santiago is a…supermodel? I burst out laughing. The thought was ludicrous.

I continued to the dorms, my mind an impossible mess. But one thing I knew, I would figure out my own housing.

I'm sure the school had somewhere for me to go, so my dad could just pound sand. I mean, what was this? The only rational explanation was that my father was some overprotective bastard who hired someone to stalk me.

When I got to the lobby, there were several housing employees handing out flyers and forms. It looked like they were putting everyone up at the visitor center until the affected rooms could be cleaned. I asked one lady about Christy, and all she could tell me was that there'd be a public statement made later and that I'd better go pack some things while I had the chance.

I took several deep breaths, bolstering myself to go upstairs. Dozens of other students carrying boxes poured out of the building.

When I got to my floor, I instantly noticed the smell of char and dampness. People milled about in the common area at the end of the hall talking about what had happened. Arson. Contraband toaster. Smoking in bed. That's what people were saying, so I guessed no one really knew. I made my way down the soggy, carpeted hallway to my room and opened the door. There was no sign of a fire, but everything was damp and had a weird smell.

I felt sick to my stomach thinking about Christy next door.

"Hey! You completely flaked on me last night! Where did you go? Why didn't you answer your cell?" Bridget staggered in, mascara smeared down her rosy face.

"Huh?" My mind snapped to. "Oh shit. I'm so sorry, Bridget. I ran into that guy, Santiago. We sort of got into a fight." I looked inside my purse and grabbed my cell. "On vibrate. Sorry." I shoved it in my pocket.

"Did you hear about our neighbor?" she asked.

"Yeah." There wasn't much to say. It was just…sad. Heartbreakingly sad.

"It sounds strange, but a part of me still hopes she'll turn up at a friend's house." She sighed loudly.

I didn't have the heart to tell her that I'd heard they took away the body.

"Well," she sighed. "Where'd you spend the night?"

"At Santiago's," I replied.

"Santiago's? Normally, I'd be squealing and asking you inappropriate questions because he's so frigging hot, but that doesn't seem right."

She had no idea just how wrong everything was. One more "un-right" thing wouldn't make a lick of a difference.

"Don't worry; you're not missing out on anything juicy." I shrugged. "Santiago and I didn't do anything—wait, where'd you spend the night?"

She smiled and made a little bow. "The fire was all over the news, so I stayed with Eric at his place." She let out a long, happy breath. "Once again, normally, I'd be oozing details and basking in the glory of my conquest, but I'm not in the mood."

There was a knock at the door and one of the coordinators popped her head in to tell us we had twenty minutes before they closed the floor.

Bridget looked around the room. "Damn. I'm going downstairs to see if they have garbage bags. Everything's sopping wet. I'll bring you a few."

I thanked her and started sorting through my damp drawers. I felt my phone buzz and checked it—my father. I ignored it and kept pulling stuff out, setting down the clothes into soggy piles on the damp bed. My phone buzzed two more times, each call sending my thumping heart into a deeper tailspin of anger. On his fourth attempt, I couldn't take it anymore. "What?"

"Dakota, don't speak. Just listen." His voice was hard and cold.

"No. You listen! I'm beyond pissed. Do you hear me? Whatever sick crap you and—"

"I'm not fucking around, Dakota. You need to listen." I'd never heard him swear at me. Not once. Not even on the rare occasion when I'd done something stupid.

"Okay." I tried to keep my voice from trembling.

"I spoke to the fire chief this morning. He said they thought the fire next door was caused by a curling iron."

"Dad, I don't underst—"

"They just called back. They found something. You need to get out of there."

"But I—"

"Santiago is on his way. Do as he says. Do you hear me?"

"Dad, please…you need to tell me what's going on."

"Baby, I love you. Just…stay with Santiago until I come for you. He'll keep you safe."

The knock at the door was so loud that I jumped.

"Safe from who?" I asked, but the call had ended.

Santiago burst through the door, panting. "Why didn't you answer?" he blurted, and then noticed the look of horror on my face. His chest expanded with a deep breath. "It's going to be fine. I promise."

He walked over, gripped me by the shoulders, and then hugged me. I supposed it was obvious that my mental state was on the fragile side.

Santiago pulled back and his demeanor suddenly shifted from human being to man on a mission. "You can cry in the car if you need to, but it's time to go."

I felt too terrified to cry. "Where are we going?"

"Somewhere safe," he replied.

"For how long?" I asked.

"As long as it takes."

"Who are we running from?"

"Very, very bad people," he replied.

I somehow sensed my life really did depend on Santiago now. I didn't like the feeling of being so vulnerable and weak.

I reached for my purse.

"You can't take anything with you," he said.

"Why not?"

He grabbed the phone in my hand and threw it onto the sopping wet floor. "Your identity has been compromised. There might be devices planted on your things."

Compromised? Devices? Those were words used by shady spies. "This is not happening."

He growled impatiently. "Yes. It is. Now deal with it."

I protested with a hiss. "I need a few things. Underwear, socks—"

"Fine, but…" he looked at the trash can and emptied the moist, crumpled pieces of paper on the floor. He handed me the white plastic shopping bag. "Use this."

I held the slightly grubby bag in my hand. "I've got an overnight bag. It might be dry—"

He shot an angry, impatient glance my way and then marched over to the door. He quickly peered into the hall. "You will use the bag. You have exactly five seconds."

Shit. I turned the bag inside out, scooped a pile of clothes from the bottom drawer of my dresser, and shoved them inside. They smelled funny but were actually dry. Then I saw my notebook peeking out from beneath the wet pillow. I snatched it up and checked the thing. It was lightly damp on the outside, but fine. I shoved it into the bag between two T-shirts. "Okay. Ready," I said with a shaky voice.

Santiago grabbed my hand and walked me out of the building as if we were escaping a ticking bomb.

CHAPTER NINETEEN

"This is your car?" I asked as we approached the large, black Mercedes sedan with tinted windows, parked curbside.

"Put your seat belt on." He opened the door and waited for me to slide in before slamming it shut.

He quickly got behind the wheel and sped out of the lot. "Santiago?"

His dark eyes focused intensely on the road ahead as he weaved through the local traffic. "Not now. I'm concentrating."

When we approached the red light, his head whipped from side to side. He hit the accelerator and roared right through the intersection.

My nails dug into the black leather seats. "Holy shit. Are you trying to kill me?"

"Funny," he mumbled to himself. "The girl asks if I'm trying to kill her."

"Nothing about this is funny."

"Agreed. Now let me drive." He looked in the rearview mirror and then made a hard right.

I looked behind us, but didn't see anyone following.

He took another hard right into a parking garage and pulled into a spot next to a silver Suburban with tinted windows.

"What are we doing?" I asked, panting.

"Changing cars. What does it look like?"

He pulled a set of keys from his pocket and hit the remote. The lights on the Suburban flashed. "Get in."

He'd been planning for this. An escape with me. I couldn't begin to articulate how frightening I found that to be. Why would I, of all people, need to have an escape planned for me?

I got in the truck, and he calmly exited the garage, pulling into traffic like we had all the time in the world.

"Are we being followed?" I asked.

"No."

"How do you know?"

"It's my job to know," he replied.

"Job." I laughed, and shook my head. One more piece of the puzzle slid into place. "I'm your job. So you're some bodyguard?"

"Something like that."

"Did my dad hire you?" I asked.

"Something like that."

"Are you going to tell me anything?"

"No," he replied.

"No?" Did he really expect me to go along with all this without him telling me what was happening? "Why the hell not?"

He glanced at me, clearly annoyed. "My job is to keep you safe, not answer questions that will only make you…less safe."

"Less safe. Wow! Fucking unbelievable. You ruin my life, and I get riddles."

"Don't start," he warned.

"Screw you."

He huffed. "Nice."

"What do you expect me to say? Oh, thank you, Santiago. Thank you for stalking me, making me think I'm crazy, and then tearing me away from my life without so much as an explanation as to why I'm being subjected to…your *job*?"

"Ask your father," he replied coldly.

"He's not here. Otherwise, trust me, I would."

We pulled onto the freeway, and Santiago's dark eyes continued scanning the mirrors.

"So," I said, "are you going to tell me who you are and why you've been stalking me?"

"I told you. It's my job. I work for your father. But let's get one thing straight: I never asked for this assignment. You," he glanced my way, "chose me."

"Care to elaborate?"

"The photo."

Oh. My brain ran a couple of queasy laps. *I picked out a photo. I put it on Facebook. My dad saw it. Poof. Santiago.* No, the pieces still weren't forming an explanation of any sort.

I ran my hands over my clammy face. "I'm guessing my father isn't the photographer who took your picture. Probably isn't a photographer at all."

"No," he said.

"And you're not a model," I said.

"No."

"Is your name even Santiago?"

"No. That's the name you made up. My name is Paolo. I'm actually Italian, not Spanish." I hadn't noticed before—too busy going out of my mind, I supposed—but his accent had changed.

He hit the fast lane, but kept the speed under eighty.

"Well, that's a start. And my dad, what is he? Some spy? An assassin? Do you work for the CIA?"

Paolo continued concentrating on the road. "No."

"Then what?"

"We keep an eye on things and we gather information. There is no name for us," he said, his accent now completely unmasked. *Der iz no name for usss…* "We don't exist."

Jeez. Well, that explains oh so very much! "Have you been trained in the fine art of not answering questions?"

"Maybe."

"You're unbelievable."

He sighed. "I'm not trying to be an asshole, but that's all you're getting. My job is to keep you alive. Not to make you feel better or answer your questions. If that were the case, I'd never get a day off."

What a jerk!

"For the record," I said. "You don't need to try."

"Try what?"

"Being an azzzhole," I said, mocking his accent. "It comes naturally."

He grumbled something in Italian under his breath and focused on the road. I suddenly wished I'd taken a foreign language—specifically, Italian. Because whatever he'd said, it sounded mean.

I sank into my seat and looked out the window to my right, trying to process the drastic turn my life had just taken. Sadly, so many things began to make sense, while others made less and less. My father's constant distance from me and my mother, for example. Had it been to keep us safe from whatever crap he was mixed up in? Now that I thought about it, he did act pretty shady. Sometimes he'd fly in unexpectedly in the middle of the night, always bringing some stranger with him who he'd introduce as a "business associate."

"Oh my God!" I snapped my fingers. "That's where I've seen you before! You were his driver." A few years ago, my father had come for a quick one-day visit on my birthday. As a gift, he took me shopping. I remembered how odd it seemed that his chauffeur followed us around in the mall. Santiago—Paolo—*was* some sort of bodyguard. My only question: Did he protect me from criminals or work for one? Or both? Anything seemed possible at this point.

"You remember me?" he asked, sounding surprised.

"Why are you so shocked?"

"You didn't look at me that day. Not once. You were too busy glaring at your father."

I remembered now. It was right after I'd spotted my dad in San Francisco with that other woman. But, of course, Paolo knew all about that. Didn't he?

"Yeah. It was a pretty shitty day," I said under my breath.

"I know. I'm sorry."

"Apparently not that sorry because you used that little tidbit of info to blackmail me into following along with your sick little game."

"Like I said," he replied briskly, "I'm sorry. But your father wasn't actually doing what you think."

"You expect me to believe that?" I asked. "Because I know what I saw."

He didn't respond.

"Let me guess. I should ask my father?"

He nodded. "Yes."

"So is my mother in on this?" Although I found it hard to believe she would subject me to all this—it didn't fit her overprotective, for-the-good-of-humanity personality—I had to ask. Also, when Santiago first appeared in my life, she'd acted like she'd just met him. Frankly, my mother was a horrible liar, so I knew she wasn't faking.

"Yes, she knows," he replied.

What? It was official. The entire world had betrayed me. But why? "You're trying to tell me that my mother knew who you were the moment you showed up?" I asked.

"No. But…it's complicated. You need to ask—"

"My father." I felt my face turn a frustrated shade of red.

"Dakota, I can't give you any information. It would be different if you weren't my boss's daughter, but you are. He's given me strict instructions not to tell you anything that isn't directly related to saving your life. Satisfying your curiosity doesn't qualify."

"What a jerk," I fumed.

He ignored me and continued watching the road like a well-trained robot.

We continued up Highway 15 for about thirty minutes and then exited and jumped on a back road. We continued north, driving in a charged, uncomfortable silence. I looked at his phone sitting on the console, wondering when my father might call or if "Santiago" would let me contact my mother. Not that my parents ever bothered calling me back.

"Can you at least tell me if my mother's safe?"

"I don't know. My job is you. Not her."

Job. There was that word again. My life was a mess, but he referred to it in the same impersonal way a janitor might talk about cleaning floors. At the end of the day, he could go home, pop open a cold one, and watch the game.

"Nice bedside manner there, *Paolo*. When can I call her?"

"You can't."

"I can't ever call her?"

"Not until the situation is…resolved."

"But, of course, you have no clue when that will be."

"No," he replied.

"Well, it's still a free country, and I'm an adult." I reached for the phone, but he pushed my hand away. He quickly popped the battery and chucked the device out the window.

What the hell? "Such impressive eco-friendly manners there, bub, but you and my father can't keep me prisoner," I snapped.

He nodded. "I suppose you're right."

"You mean you're not going to argue the point?"

"What's to argue?" he said briskly. "You can leave anytime you like. If you're willing to accept the consequences."

The car made a sharp turn left and then right as we wound our way up the mountain road. Funny, the day looked so clear and bright, the sky a pristine blue. The weather inside the vehicle, however, felt closer to a thunderstorm.

The eye of the rabbit hole…

"Such as?" I asked.

"Your death. Possibly mine if I don't keep you safe."

What? "You're not insinuating my father would kill you. That's absurd."

"Is it now?" he replied.

Okay. Maybe it wasn't. I had no clue what sort of man my father was. Come to think of it, hadn't he met my mother because he'd been shot? Lord, he was probably some sort of gangster.

"Your father actually *would* kill me," he added, "but only for one thing: touching you. However, what I meant was that if you run and these assholes really know who you are, they will track you down within a few days. I'd have to come rescue you, which would be pointless because you'd be dead already—your head shipped off to your father—but I'd come looking for you anyway. My head would follow."

His head, too? He couldn't be serious. "Silver linings...aren't they just magical?"

"Crack all the jokes you want, but I guarantee the only thing that has kept you alive all these years is that those people don't know you exist. If that veil of protection is gone, then welcome to your new fucking life." He pointed to himself.

No. No way.

"You can't really expect me to believe all this crap?" Not that Santi—*shit*—Paolo had actually told me anything other than I was in danger and my father wasn't who I thought.

"Believe anything you like. Just don't get in the way of my job," he said without emotion.

Crap. So this is what it all came down to? I would get no answers, but I'd get to choose either doing everything he told me, leaving my life behind, and going into hiding; or refusing to listen to him and taking the risk that he was full of shit about me being dead in a few days. Those were my choices? Really? Really?

"Pull over," I demanded.

"What?"

"I said pull over! I'm going to be sick."

He pulled into a narrow turnout, and I exited the vehicle, bolting for a stand of tall pines. I leaned into one, attempting to eject the burning knots, but there was nothing to throw up since I hadn't eaten. My last meal had been before the party the previous evening. That didn't stop my stomach, however, from trying to relinquish the pit of despair inside.

"You okay?" Paolo appeared from behind, gripping my shoulders.

I turned and looked up at him. His thick layer of black stubble made his lips stand out as if being presented on a silver platter. And the whites of his dark eyes, though slightly red, likely from a lack of sleep, still captivated me. Something fierce lurked inside his gaze, a sort of dissonance and anger—stubbornness that spoke volumes about who he really was.

He stared down at me and brushed a few strands of hair from my face, but then quickly dropped his hand. "You look hungry."

I nodded dumbly.

"Maybe getting a little food in you will settle your stomach."

He walked back toward the road, and I followed, carefully stepping over fallen branches until I reached the SUV.

Once inside, I noticed that Paolo's eyes were locked on the empty road ahead. "What's wrong?" I asked.

He snapped out of it. "Nothing. Was just thinking."

"About?" I asked.

He blew out a breath. "I'm sure we won't hear from your father for a few days, maybe a week."

"A week?" I asked, my tone mildly panicked.

"Afraid of being alone with me for that long?" His eyes dropped to my chest but promptly returned to my face.

I felt the tremor return to my stomach, but it wasn't fear. "Maybe."

"Good answer."

Why had he said that? Did he want me to be afraid of him?

"Okaaay," I sighed. "Any thoughts on how my dad is going to contact us if we don't have phones?"

"Don't worry," he grumbled. "We have our ways."

I wasn't sure what their "ways" were, but I had no choice now but to hope this would be over quickly.

An hour later, Paolo stopped at a small mom-and-pop convenience store to pick up supplies—food, toothbrushes, soap, etc. At the checkout, he pulled a huge wad of cash from his jeans, and, naturally, I stared. I'd never seen so much money. And while my eyes were down there, and my mind was a complete mess, they stopped to stare at his other wad.

"Eh-hem," he said.

My head snapped up. *Oh my God.* I looked away and followed him to the car, embarrassed as hell that I'd been caught ogling his crotch.

"Where are we going?" I wanted to push my thoughts to a less uncomfortable place.

"There's a cabin just up the road. There are no phones or Internet, so there's no risk of you contacting someone you shouldn't in a moment of weakness."

He knew me too well.

બ્જ્જ

Not long after the pit stop, we turned down a narrow dirt road that was lined with tall pine trees and led us to a rickety gate with a padlock. It looked like the scene of a horror movie waiting to happen. Once deeper inside the property, however, the quaint two-story cabin came into view. It was dark brown with a pitched roof and a large porch.

"Are we safe here?" I asked, thinking not only about the humans, but the animals, too.

"Nothing to be afraid of, except not listening to me." He smiled warmly, as if to comfort me. I guessed that we were now in familiar territory, since Paolo felt more at ease. It instantly showed because "Robot Paolo" had retreated.

The interior of the cabin, though kind of dark from the wood-paneled walls and plank wood floors, was cozy with a rustic charm—large, overstuffed plaid couch, wood burning stove, neatly folded quilts, and antique ski gear on the walls. The living room had a small dining table off in the corner, and a large open doorway separated it from the small kitchen area.

Paolo unloaded the grocery bags into the cupboards and fridge while I stood in the living room, checking out his collection of books on the mantel. Homer's *Odyssey*, Hemingway's *The Sun Also Rises*...

Pride and Prejudice?

"Whose place is this?" I asked.

"Mine. I come here when I need to decompress."

A man who decompresses with Austen and *Hemingway?* I wasn't certain how to reconcile that thought, so I didn't try.

133

"So you live in California then?" I asked, also thinking how odd that would be. Of all the photos of all the men in the world I could've picked, I chose a guy who worked for my dad and lived in my state.

"I spend most of my time in California, when I'm not working," he replied.

Must be fate.

Idiot.

"So *they* won't find us here?" I asked. Whoever "they" were.

He glanced at me through the large doorway, with an irritated twitch in his eyes.

"Sorry." I held up my palms. "Didn't mean to doubt you, mighty one."

I went to explore a bit but there wasn't much to see. There was a loft-style bedroom upstairs. Downstairs had a bath, another small bedroom, the kitchen, and the living room.

"I didn't take you as a cabin man, Paolo," I called out, coming down the stairs.

"I am a man of many mysteries." He came out of the kitchen with a hand towel over his shoulder. "Such as, I love to cook."

"Italian food?" I asked.

"How did you guess?" He went back to his cooking, and I watched him from the doorway.

"I have my *ways*," I responded jokingly.

He laughed and uncorked a bottle of red wine on the kitchen counter and poured himself a glass.

"What other mysteries can you share?" I asked.

He gave it a moment of thought. "I grew up in a very small town in Italy. Moved to the States for college."

"What did you study?" I asked.

"International Relations."

"So how did you meet my dad?"

"Mr. Dane recruited me. But it wasn't for my IR knowledge; it was for my political connections—my family is fairly…well known. It didn't hurt that I have a passion for technology and am an expert marksman."

"Military training?" I asked.

"My grandfather was big on hunting. He took me to shoot game every summer."

I cringed. That did not sound appealing, but I wasn't about to complain about the being handy with a gun thing.

"Of course," he added, "I've had much more training now."

He dumped a bag of dry pasta into a pot of boiling water, and I watched his back as he stirred. The way his insanely broad shoulders moved and stretched under his T-shirt and the way his back tapered down into a tight waist caught my eye. I couldn't help but admire his perfect male form.

"Are you staring at my ass again?" he asked.

Oh God. How embarrassing.

I cleared my throat. "How did you know?"

"I can see your reflection in my glass right there." He nodded toward his wine on the counter.

"Ah. Well…"

He turned with a stern look on his face. "Dakota, I need to be clear with you. I'm not having sex with you."

I blinked. Was he for real? It wasn't like I had been coming on to him. And if he thought I had been, why did he insist on addressing it with such an "in your face" approach? He'd said almost the exact same thing back when he'd been my high school "boyfriend," and it was just as weird then as it was now. What was his deal?

Maybe he wants to clear the air. After all, you woke up this morning with your hand wrapped around his penis and you have sexual fantasies about him almost every night.

Damn it. Could he tell I was sexually attracted to him? If yes, did he understand that it was despite my better judgment? I was only human and, whether I liked it or not, the man was, in fact, the most gorgeous male I'd ever seen. That didn't mean that I liked his personality or wanted to throw myself at him. I was smarter than lust.

"It's normal," he said, "to develop feelings for someone who protects you in a dangerous situation."

"I looked at your ass," I barked. "I did not ask you to sleep with me."

"I realize that, but you might. We're going to be here for a week, and I don't want you to misinterpret my intentions. I'm here to protect you. Not get you into bed. This is work. Nothing else."

"You know what? I think *you're* the one who sounds worried. What? Afraid you'll throw yourself at me in a moment of weakness?" I asked, half-serious, half not.

His gaze was frigid. "I know how to handle myself on the job."

Job. Job. Yes, that was an excellent reminder of why I should shoo away any lustful thoughts from my mind. I was nothing but an assignment he'd move on from once this was over.

"Well," I said in a suggestive tone just to mess with him, letting my eyes roam over his body, "I'll be the judge of how well you handle yourself."

"Dakota, I'm serious. There can't be any of that between us."

"Oh my God. I was kidding. I'm surprised that your giant ego actually fits inside that head. How did you manage to squeeze it all in?" I snagged the bottle off the counter.

"Where are you going with that?"

"Outside," I answered, marching to the front porch.

"You're underage."

I held up my middle finger, but I'd already turned the corner so he couldn't see.

"I saw that!" he said.

Damn it! The guy was like a goddamned spider with eyes stuck all over his giant fat head!

"I can see your reflection in the windshield of the truck," he added.

Of course, it was parked out front.

I dusted off the rocking chair on the porch and took a sip from the bottle. It was actually quite nice. I'd never tried red wine, but the sweetness mixed with a tart aftertaste was perrrty yummy.

The screen door creaked and Paolo appeared with two glasses.

"I sense you are new to drinking wine. It tastes better with one of these."

"Har, har." I took the glass and filled it halfway.

He leaned against the rail, directly in front of me. "I am sorry about my bluntness. You must think I am a heartless asshole." It was funny how his Italian accent sounded so thick now. Was this the real Paolo?

I didn't reply, but took a sip from my glass instead.

"Okay," he said. "You win. I will fuck you. But only if you don't tell your father."

"What?" I snapped my head in his direction, finding a giant grin stretched across his face. "Funny." Actually, it sort of was. I started to laugh. Laughing felt good.

He tilted his head. "You have a lovely smile."

"Are you flirting with me? Because if you are, it won't work. I'm not sleeping with you."

He laughed, and it was a deep, sexy, habit-forming laugh.

I couldn't look away—wouldn't have been able to even if a bear had popped out of the woods wearing a hula skirt. "You have a n—n—nice laugh, too." I sipped my wine to unstick that glob in my throat.

He looked at me, and his smile melted away. His dark eyes bore into me, and the tension between us spiked. A gust of wind hit the treetops at the same moment, as if the gods were warning us both to back off.

"I'd better finish dinner." He disappeared inside, and I released a breath I'd been unknowingly holding in.

Damn it, Dakota. What's the matter with you?

Somewhere out there, a group of people wanted to hunt me down and ship my head off in a box to my father. And here I was, getting worked up over the man who saw me as work—a project he'd leave behind once his next assignment came along—whose scruples answered to a higher power (my father), and whose sense of right and wrong were dictated by a world that existed only in the shadows, a world I knew nothing about but had suddenly become a part of.

I took another sip and gazed into the forest, wondering where this story would end.

Can't be a good place.

CHAPTER TWENTY

After a relatively silent dinner peppered with a few polite comments and smiles (and quite possibly the most exquisite pasta I'd ever sampled—diced onions, mushrooms, and bits of crispy bacon mixed with a creamy sauce, poured over fettuccine), I washed the dishes while Santi—Paolo went outside to do whatever crap international men of mystery did. Set up booby-traps, load guns, let off some steam by killing something large and fury...I didn't know. But when he came inside shirtless, mopping his brow with his tee, panting and sweating, frankly, I didn't care.

The plate in my hand went crashing to the floor along with my jaw. *Good move, Dakota.*

"Let me help you with that." He grabbed a broom and dustpan from a small closet next to the front door.

I reached for them, and when my hands touched his, he froze.

I tugged the broom handle toward me. "I've got it, really."

He stared for several long moments, giving me a brutally carnal look that made me quiver in my flip-flops.

No. I must be imagining it. He'd clearly said I was a job, and he was off-limits.

I cleared my dry throat. "Did you want to say something?"

He blinked as if I'd broken a magical entrancement. "I...I'm going to take a shower. Thank you for washing dishes." He sauntered off, and though I was certain he could see my expression reflected in some hidden spoon strategically positioned somewhere in the room, I didn't care. The goddamned man smelled like fresh sweat. He looked like an indestructible pillar of bulging, blatant masculinity. And when he walked away, all I could see was a towering mass of lust-provoking maleness. All I could think of was how we'd woken up this morning with our legs intertwined, my hand on his abundantly proportioned, hard-as-steel erection.

I sighed. "God save me," I whispered. "Couldn't my dad have picked someone old, short, and bald?"

I quickly finished off the dishes and went into the bedroom, hoping to find a large shirt to sleep in. I didn't think the tiny tee, pair of pink socks, and panties I'd brought with me would do the trick.

I opened the top dresser drawer and found... "Shit! A really, really large automatic handgun..." I picked it up. It looked like the kind of gun Rambo might own. I carefully slid it back, glancing over my shoulder at the bathroom door. Paolo's deep voice rang out, as he sang something in Italian.

Opera. I couldn't help but smile. He was so...Italian.

I slid open the next drawer and saw a pink lacy nightie along with some other clothing. I held it up and inspected the garment with curiosity.

"If you need something to sleep in, my T-shirts are one drawer down."

Paolo stood in the doorway, dripping wet, a white towel wrapped around his waist. His well-defined pecs and biceps were just as astoundingly sinful as the last time I'd seen them, ten minutes ago. At least I thought it was ten minutes. Who knows how long I had been standing there gawking at the nightie?

I placed the nightgown back in the drawer and attempted to hide my emotions. What shocked me most was how much I didn't want to think about him with someone else. It sparked a raging case of jealousy. But that couldn't be right, unless Paolo had been correct—that when people are in dangerous situations, they quickly grow attachments to those who protect them.

Quickly? Quickly? I challenged myself. *You've thought of nothing but him for the last five months.*

Okay. Maybe I did feel something slightly deeper than good old-fashioned lust. But I couldn't say exactly what it was. Not when anger, resentment, and suspicion were thrown into the soup.

But I couldn't deny I felt jealous, which was plain stupid. Paolo had to be in his early to mid-twenties. He'd probably had quite a few girlfriends. Maybe one in every city. After all, he was an international man of mystery and not some college freshman virgin—a unicorn—like me.

"Thanks," I said, and found a white T-shirt in the next drawer down.

"You can sleep in this bed. I'll take the couch down here," he said.

"What's wrong with the bed upstairs?" I asked.

"I'll rest easier down here, closer to you," was all he offered.

Hadn't he said we were safe here? If he believed it, then there was no reason for him to be on the couch.

I was about to say something, but realized I didn't want to push him upstairs. Hell, I wanted him to sleep next to me.

"Okay." I nodded and headed for the bathroom, avoiding the tempting view as I passed. I didn't want to see him half-naked. Not when I needed to avoid fueling my irrational feelings for him. Besides—not that I wanted him—he was something I could never have. I'd never be the owner of that negligee. Not in his eyes. I was merely the boss's daughter. A girl.

A...job.

～◌〜◌

Over the next two days, I could have sworn the universe was trying to torture me. Well, that or Paolo. Although, he kept his distance doing work around the cabin, chopping wood (shirtless for God's sake) or patrolling the property, every time we got anywhere near each other he looked like he wanted to devour me, which sent me into a spiral of unsanctioned lustful thoughts, which shut down all brain function. Then his gaze would run the whole gamut of aggressive expressions—irritation, anger, frustration, and disgust—leaving me feeling like a sad little puddle of unrequited lust. Then we'd both retreat to our corners.

When we ate, he avoided eye contact almost completely. When I asked him if he had any news, he simply answered "no" and then disappeared outside or upstairs.

I didn't know what the hell was going on inside that man's head, but I couldn't spend another day, let alone another week, like this.

On the third evening, I sat on the couch, trying to look casual, curled up with a cup of tea and a book—don't even know which damned book—waiting for his return from a perimeter sweep.

When he entered the front door, I immediately knew he'd been running or doing pull-ups on a tree branch or lifting boulders, because once again the goddamned man wore no shirt—only a pair of black drawstring shorts—and glistened with sweat. His biceps, abs, and forearms bulged with tension.

He stood in the doorway, his angry-as-fuck gaze drilling into me, his fists flexing.

I swallowed and felt the heat surge between my legs. I don't know what it was about this man, but his smell, the sound of his breath, the mere deliciousness of being in his presence completely messed with my head.

I cleared my throat. "Hi."

"Hi," he replied coldly.

"We need to talk."

He cocked one brow and then slammed the door behind him. "Stop looking at me like that."

"Like what?" With my shaking hand, I set the book down next to my tea on the table in front of me.

"Like that," he said with a tinge of disgust. "You're driving me fucking crazy. It won't work."

"What?" I resisted standing up, and took a calming breath. "Paolo, I am not trying to do anything."

"Do I look like a fucking idiot?" he seethed.

"I don't know what you—"

"You're beautiful, Dakota. Your body is a piece of fucking art, but that doesn't mean you can use it to get what you want."

Huh? "Which is?"

His gaze lowered to my chest and then elevated back to my eyes. "We both know you want to call your mother."

"True, but…"

"I bet you're used to getting what you want. But I'm not some fucking hard up college guy. I'm trying to do my job here. I'm trying to keep you safe, and every time you flirt with me or show off your body, you're only distracting me."

Holy shit. He thought I was trying to distract him with T-shirts and his loaner jogging shorts? Sure, I wasn't wearing a bra and had to roll the waist down so the shorts would stay on, but…"I'm not the one prancing around shirtless and showing off my giant muscles, Paolo. Seriously. Do you ever stop working out? How fucking big is your ego if you need to pump iron every hour?"

He growled. "I'm only blowing off steam. Steam that would otherwise go toward taking you to that bed and fucking you senseless which would only get us both killed." He turned and yanked open the front door, disappearing into the night.

I blew out a long, hot breath and then gripped the sides of my head. His stark, sexual words sent my entire body into a raging frenzy. Just hearing him say those things conjured images I'd never be able to dispel. Ever. And knowing that he'd been having his own lustful thoughts only made mine all the more potent.

"Holy shit, Dakota. What are you doing?"

Playing with fire. That's what.

I didn't think I'd been trying to seduce him. After all, we were talking about me. But maybe he was right; I wanted him to want me. And it didn't matter what my brain said, the pull he had over my body was ten times more powerful.

I needed to get a grip.

The hot shower worked miracles on my mental composure. Having clean hair and freshly shaved legs—

hoped he didn't mind me borrowing his razor—almost made me feel new again. I toweled off, slipped on fresh panties and another of Paolo's tee. It smelled like cedar and Tide. I tried to ignore how charming and domesticated that seemed.

I peeked out the bathroom door, and not seeing my ghost in question, I figured I could slip into bed without any issue. But when I entered the bedroom, he was there putting something in the closet.

"Oh, sorry," I turned away to find something to cover myself with, leaving my ass on display. Fact: Dakota Dane only owned thongs. Fact: They weren't nearly as comfortable as bikinis or boy shorts. Fiction: My ego was above wearing extra-large panties despite having no one to show my panties to.

"Dakota."

"Are you looking at my ass?" I said jokingly, trying to hide behind humor when the reality was that having his eyes on me felt so good.

"Yes. Yes I am," he replied. "And if you don't want me to get killed, you'd do me a favor and put that thing away."

I nodded slowly and then faced him. His hungry eyes met mine, and though my mind knew this would go nowhere, I couldn't help but want it.

"You're so," he whispered, "beautiful. I don't think I've ever seen a more beautiful woman."

I didn't know what to say. His words were like fuel for that insane part of my head that wanted him despite the wrongness.

No. You're reacting to the stress of the situation. Don't do it, Dakota.

Shut up.

I slid the towel off my hair and walked over to him, leaving only inches between our bodies. "What you said earlier…about blowing off steam. I thought you said you didn't want to sleep with me."

Towering over me, he placed his hands on my waist and gazed down with that magnificent, masculine face. Jaw, cheekbones, nose…every inch of him was perfect. And in the short period of time we'd spent together, I was beginning to see he was more than just a pretty picture. There was a deep sense of loyalty and dedication lurking in there. The question was, did he feel those things for me or for my father?

"I never said I didn't want to," he responded in a gravelly voice. "I said I wouldn't."

"That's very disappointing," I said. "Because I can't think of anyone I'd rather have for my first time."

I can't believe I said that! How…cheesy! And where had my sudden burst of "seductressness" come from?

His eyes flickered. Was he shocked? Disgusted? Turned on? "How much wine did you drink?" he asked.

"Not nearly enough." Especially if he took me up on my offer. I'd touched him that one morning and now felt his penis pressing firmly against my stomach. He wasn't small.

"Dakota," he lowered his forehead to mine and cupped the back of my head. "You don't want this. I don't do relationships. And there's a reason for that. It's too…dangerous."

I pulled back. "You're really that frightened of my father?"

He shook his head slowly, not breaking our eye contact. "No. He doesn't frighten me."

"Then what?"

His eyes flashed to the dresser, and my mind connected another dot.

Christ. "Who is she?" I asked.

"She died a year before I met you."

I stepped back. "I'm so sorry."

"It's in the past. But we are bound to repeat it if we don't learn from our mistakes." His hands dropped to his side.

What mistake did he mean? "You can't think that loving someone is a mistake."

Again, he seemed surprised. "No. I…I don't think loving her was a mistake. But I won't watch someone die because she loved me back."

So he'd had something to do with her death? I was about to ask, but the despair in his eyes was too much to bear. I could tell he wasn't even close to getting over whatever had happened. Perhaps, it was the sort of thing no one ever got over. I didn't know, and I never wanted to find out.

"I'm sure she didn't regret a moment of it," I offered. "I know I wouldn't."

His eyes went from hard to soft to hard again. "Good night, Dakota."

He went to the couch, and I slipped into his flannel sheets, wondering how this man I barely knew suddenly felt like the center of my universe and the path to my destruction.

CHAPTER TWENTY-ONE

"Dakota." Paolo's deep masculine voice stretched into my dreams, grabbed me by the collar, and yanked me violently into the here and now. "Wake the hell up," he whispered.

My eyes opened to Paolo's face inches from mine, the warm glow of flames behind him, the smell of a fire filling my nose.

Crap. I sat up and looked toward the curtained window. The blaze was outside.

"Look at me, Dakota."

I did.

"We can't run outside. It's a trap. They'll be waiting to pick us off."

Oh my God. "They found us? But how?"

"I don't know," he said. He reached and grabbed something from the nightstand and put it on his head—some sort of visor. He already had a rifle strapped to his back.

"The cabin is on fire. We'll burn alive," I shrieked.

"No we won't." He opened that middle drawer—the one with that woman's clothes—and threw a pair of jeans at me. "Put those on." I was in no position to complain about wearing his deceased lover's clothes, so I did as he said, but that didn't mean I enjoyed it. He handed me my flip-flops next. "I wish you'd brought tennis shoes, but they'll have to do."

"I thought you said we weren't running."

"Not yet." He grabbed my hand, pulled me to the bathroom, and shoved me under the showerhead. "Wet yourself down." He turned the handle, and cold water torpedoed my face.

"Shit!" I said as I saw him dart into the other room. "Wait. Don't go!" Panicked, I stepped out onto the floor, but he came right back.

He turned off the shower and then gripped me hard by the shoulders. "Dakota, I know this is going to be difficult, but I want you to lie inside the tub. Cover you head with a towel. Wait here—do not move until I come back for you. Got it?"

He shoved me back inside the bathtub and pushed me down.

"Where are you going?"

"To the roof." He grabbed something from his waistband and placed it in my hands. "If anyone, besides me—key word *besides*—comes in here, shoot. Don't stop to ask any questions. Just shoot. The safety is already off. " I looked at the weapon. It was a small black handgun. I'd never touched a gun in my life, let alone fired one, but I got the gist of how it worked. How different could it be from a video arcade? But would I really be able to shoot another person?

If your life depends on it? Absolutely.

"You'll be back, right?" The cabin continued to fill with smoke and orange light poured in from the windows through the living room. We couldn't have more than just a few minutes before the entire place burned down with us inside.

He looked at me and brushed the wet hair from my face. "I'll be back. I promise." He kissed my forehead and disappeared. I heard his footsteps thump up the stairs. And then the waiting started. I tried to calm my breathing, but the air was thickening. I lowered myself down a little farther in the tub, hoping the extra few inches would provide more breathable air. It did. But damn it, what if he didn't come back? What if the fire got so bad that there was no way to get out? All of the exits would be blocked, if they weren't already.

Shit. I can't believe this is happening.

I heard a loud *pop, pop, pop.*

I held my breath, listening for the sound of Paolo's footsteps coming down the stairs. Instead, I heard the sound of glass shattering in the living room, and then another *pop*.

Oh God. Please let him be okay. Please.

I suddenly realized how much I didn't want to lose him. It had to be just because we were in a life-and-death situation. Right? I didn't truly know, but the only thing that seemed to matter was his not dying.

"Please, please, please live. I'll do anything you want, just let him live." I'd never been the praying type, but I guessed it was human nature to roll the dice when all other avenues of salvation were null and void.

"Are you actually praying for me? I have to say, that's very sweet." Paolo's large, recognizable silhouette appeared in the doorway.

The air whooshed from my lungs. "Thank God." I put the gun down, and he grabbed my hand, plucking me out of the tub like a tiny doll. "What happened?"

"I only saw one person. He was positioned out front."

"Did you shoot him?" I asked

"Yeah. But I didn't kill him. He ran off."

Paolo dragged me through the kitchen. The fire blazed around the exterior of the cabin, including the back porch where a four-foot wall of flames greeted us when he opened the backdoor.

"We have to jump through it," he said.

Was he nuts? "You want me to run through that?" We'd be burned alive.

He grabbed the teakettle from the stove and emptied it down the front of his body. Then he shoved his head under the sink and wet down his hair.

Yes. Please save the hair. It was, after all, very, very nice hair.

He then grabbed a quilt from the couch, shoved as much as he could under the sink and dampened it.

"It's not as bad as it looks," he said. "I saw from the roof."

He pulled me to come with him.

"I can't."

He stopped and looked down at me with his dark eyes. "I promise, I won't ever let anything happen to you."

I nodded like a fool, knowing that the word "ever" was a lie. But I appreciated the conviction in his voice. He was asking me to trust him. Really, truly trust him. The ironic part was that he didn't have to ask. I already did.

"Okay." I glanced at the counter and saw my small bag of clothes lying there. *My notebook.* I grabbed it and shoved it into the back of my jeans right before he threw the quilt over the flames, grabbed my hand, and pulled me outside.

I yelped when I felt the heat, but as he'd promised, nothing happened. We came out on the other side within a split second. We ran into the forest and kept going. I stumbled my way behind him, tripping on rocks and branches. My toes felt like ground beef—whatever that feels like.

After about twenty minutes, panting hard, we ducked behind a thick tree trunk. He pressed me against it with his body and held his hand over my mouth.

"Let me listen," he whispered in my ear.

The feel of his hard frame pinning me to the tree, his chest and hips pushing against mine, unexpectedly sparked an odd, physical reaction. It was like all that adrenaline coursing through my blood had ignited, sending a blaze of sexual need right through me. I remembered reading about that kind of stuff happening to men, that when they were in the heat of battle, their testosterone levels shot through the roof and made them hornier than hell. But I didn't know that happened to women.

Paolo squeezed my shoulder, warning me not to squirm, only furthering the sensation of impending combustion despite the dampness of my cold clothes.

All too aware of what his touch was doing, I tried to wriggle to the side just a little.

"Hold still. I'm trying to listen for footsteps," he said.

Did he realize he was doing so much, much more than that? And did he realize that I wasn't the only person feeling a little frisky?

I clamped my eyes shut and tried not think about his thick, hard erection pushing against me. With the adrenaline pumping through my veins, I wanted him so badly that nothing else seemed to matter—not that someone had just tried to kill us, or that I was wet and freezing—just our bodies pressed together.

"Paolo. You need to let me go."

"I'm shielding you with my body," he argued.

"I realize that, but—"

"I don't hear anything, but I need to be sure no one is following."

"Okay, but when you're done making sure, I'd like it noted that I would prefer to lose my virginity lying down. Something soft against my back might be good, too," I lied. Christ, I'd let him have me over a heap of broken branches.

"What the hell are you—?" his head snapped down, and then he realized just what I'd meant, but he didn't step back. Instead, he simply stared. The faint light of the moon, filtering through the treetops, allowed me to see the contours of his face, but not his eyes.

Was he embarrassed? Annoyed?

He leaned his head down and kissed me. It wasn't a gentle kiss; it was forceful and demanding. His mouth moved over mine, and his tongue slipped inside, stroking me, heating me. I moved my arms around his neck and angled my head to the side, allowing him to deepen the kiss, to fit our bodies more snugly together. Blood rushed between my legs and to my nipples. The blaze of sensual need charged through my veins and consumed every rational thought I had.

A tiny groan escaped his lips as he pushed his hips more tightly against mine.

Oh God, I'd never felt anything so good.

One hand reached for my leg and lifted it as his hot mouth moved to a frantic pace, his tongue lapping away at my own. He angled himself and pushed forward again, the ridge of his hard shaft hitting me right where the tension was building. The breath whooshed from my lungs as the sensation of him thrusting against me drove the tension higher, and the need to release it to a point I could no longer bear.

His other hand moved up inside my damp shirt and cupped my breast, while he continued the erotic rhythm of his pumping hips, his tongue moving in time.

"You're so fucking beautiful, Dakota," he panted, massaging and squeezing my bare breast.

Oh my God. I'd never wanted anything more in my life. I'd never *needed* anything more than I did him at that exact moment. I slid my hand between our bodies and reached for the top button of his jeans. I worked it open, and then undid the next one. The tip of my finger grazed the velvety tip of his erection, causing him to release a groan. I slid my hand inside just a bit farther, wanting to wrap my fingers around the fullness of him.

He rocked himself into my hand and started unbuttoning the top of my jeans.

We were going to do this. Right there.

He began to slide down my pants and panties over my hips. All I could think of was getting him inside me. "You were right; I can't believe how much I want you," I said.

He froze and quickly moved back.

"It's okay," I whispered. "Don't stop." I could handle anything, anything in this world except him stopping.

"Shit. What the fuck am I doing?" He put himself back inside his jeans.

Still panting, I stood there, not caring that the rough tree bark dug into my back. "It's okay."

He turned his back to me. "It's not okay. I swear you'll be the death of me—I can't think straight around you. Button your pants."

Wounded and humiliated, I did as he asked, all the while, thinking about what a total jerk I was for letting myself get carried away like I had.

But clearly you want him. Yes. I did. In a bad way. Like I occasionally needed chocolate or to spend over my credit limit. But I was better than a simple urge. Wasn't I?

Maybe I was. Maybe I wasn't. But that didn't make the sting of rejection any less painful. Truth was, I would have gone through with it.

"Come on," he grabbed my hand and continued walking us through the woods.

"Wait." I marched back to the tree and found my notebook. Who knew, maybe this would be the only memory I'd ever have of my father after all was said and done.

Paolo cussed a few choice words and continued ahead. "Hurry, for God's sake."

We walked in silence for several moments, me wondering why he was so pissy when I was the one who'd been rejected.

"Are you actually mad?" I whispered.

He stopped abruptly, causing me to almost ram into his back. "I'm sorry."

"Sorry. Why?" I asked.

"We are in the middle of a fucking mess, and I'm acting like a fucking sixteen year old who can't keep his dick in his pants. I was unprofessional, and it will never happen again."

"Oh. That's right. I'm just a job. " I walked on ahead, not knowing where I was going, but far away from him felt insanely rational and very good.

CHAPTER TWENTY-TWO

Two long, cold hours later, I was simply thankful it was September and not October or November. Any colder and my nose, fingertips, and toes would have been left behind as ice chips.

Shivering, I watched Paolo approach a large cabin through the backyard. The lights were off. For a moment I thought he was going to break in. Instead, he walked around the side, grabbed something from a bush, and then popped open a side door leading to the attached garage.

"What are you doing?"

He waved me over.

I entered the dark garage, and he shut the door behind me. He flipped on the lights, revealing this wasn't just a garage with another SUV—this one black—but an arsenal of sorts. "Whose place is this?"

"A friend's," was his only answer.

He went quickly to work, opening locked cabinets and loading duffel bags into the back of the truck.

"Why do I have the feeling you've been planning for this event for a very, very long time?"

He glanced at me, too busy to truly see me. "Planned, yes. Very, very long, no. I was *assigned* to you again three weeks ago."

"What's in those?"

"Supplies." He plunked a heavy box into the back of the SUV, and then grabbed another box that sort of clanked when it landed. "And a few guns with plenty of ammo."

"And where does the elusive, gun-hungry Jason plan to take me now?" I crossed my goose-bumped arms over my chest.

"Jason?" he asked.

"As in…Bourne?"

He stared blankly.

Ugh! "Never mind," I said.

"I'm taking you into hiding, to a level one safe house— we only use them when there's a problem."

"Guess this qualifies," I mumbled.

"Sometimes leaks happen, which is why when we go to one, we sever all communication with other people for months."

"Months? Why months?" And how the hell would I survive months of being alone with him? I'd be a big hot mess!

"It gives your father time to find the leak. Once he sends an all clear we can leave or go to a level two—a house with a communication system and nearby contingencies."

I immediately thought about his cabin that had burned down. Contingencies must have meant a plan B, like this one.

"Are you sure we'll be safe wherever this safe house is?"

"Yes. It's the first thing we prepare when we're assigned to a protection job."

Job. There was that word again. It stung. It implied a certain level of obligation versus free will.

"You had all this," I waved my hand toward the truck and apocalyptic stockpiles, "planned in two weeks? You must have a big team." I'd only been at college for a week, so I assumed he'd had this all ready to go before he started his "assignment."

"We never use teams; I'm the only one I know I can trust. Adding other people into the equation only increases the risk of information leaking into the wrong hands. Besides," he grunted and landed another heavy box in the trunk, "it only took three days. We've got a system. I took a week off before starting. Knew I'd need the rest—my last assignment was a rough one."

Made me start to wonder where he'd been these last months after he'd disappeared from my life. "So who was the lucky woman?"

"Lucky woman?" He breathed heavily and rested a hand on top of the next box.

"Yeah. The lucky woman who got to play bodyguard with you after you left without a trace from my life. Did you almost try to screw her against a tree, too?"

He narrowed his eyes. "Dakota, you really *are* a child."

"Child? Child! I'm being hunted here. My father is Austin Powers without the bad teeth, and the guy I spent months trying to forget just showed up in my life, only to tell me that protecting me is nothing more than a chore he gets paid for. Yet…" I swept my hands over my body. "Here I am. No cracks in my fucking armor, Mr. 007. I'm here, ready to fight for my life, taking the shitty hand you just dealt me and making the best of it! All the while, having my feelings stomped on. So please!" I poked his hard chest. "Please tell me how I am the one acting like a goddamned child?"

"I'm sorry. I shouldn't have said—"

"No. You shouldn't have. Because from where I'm sitting, the only difference between you and me is that I haven't had my Spy Kids training." I poked him again. "Yet," I added. Because I'd be signing up for the first class I could get my hands on.

Paolo was about to say something, but to his credit he shut his trap.

I loaded my freezing body into the passenger seat and shut the door.

Paolo continued loading duffel bags into the large space in the back of the Suburban, and I just had to wonder where the hell he was taking me. I hoped it would be an isolated town in Alaska where a new passport awaited me along with a new life, new heart, and new…bodyguard!

After ten more minutes, he shut the hatch and got into the driver's seat. He gripped the steering wheel and stared at the garage door for several moments. The turmoil undulating just beneath his steady facade was palpable. "Dakota, I don't expect you to understand. Or believe me. But I broke the rules once." He gripped tighter. "I wasn't the one who paid the price. When I lost her, I lost everything."

Another piece of the puzzle slid into place, and I'd almost wished he hadn't told me. Yes, it now explained why he'd acted so strange around me, but it broke my heart to hear something so tragic. And all along, I'd been getting in his face about his boundaries, which now made me feel horrible. "I'm sorry. I didn't...know," I murmured.

"How could you?"

"I should have guessed," I replied. Only people with serious baggage acted that neurotic. His behavior—hot and cold, angry and caring—screamed inner turmoil. He must have cared for her deeply. "So she died while you were protecting her?"

He didn't flinch. "Yes. And I had feelings for her, but not like I have for you."

Ouch. "I understand. I would never...expect that from anyone," I mumbled.

"You misunderstood. What I feel about you is..." He bumped his fist on the steering wheel. "Fuck, Dakota. Don't ask me to repeat my mistakes. Because," he looked at me with a sharp, soul-piercing gaze, "I couldn't handle losing you. Not you." He looked ahead and opened the garage door. "I won't watch you die."

There was nothing to say to that, other than..."All right."

He nodded, and we drove off into the night, our fates awaiting us.

~•~

The place Paolo was taking me, I learned, was special for one reason: It was a house that couldn't be tied to him, me, or anyone. It belonged to a real estate firm that rented homes to executives from abroad. Payment flowed through various companies—a phony company's overseas bank account tied to an alias, through a relocation company that farmed out the actual relo work to a third company, etc. I didn't quite get why it was untraceable, but I gathered the rental had gone through so many parties that it put a healthy distance between us and anyone looking for us.

The second thing I learned was that my father was, in fact, a very, very well-connected man.

"A passport, driver's license, and a credit card?" I said to myself, in complete shock. I looked through the rest of the envelope Paolo had given me while he pumped gas. There was also a couple thousand in cash. Strangely, it looked like the large white envelope the policeman in San Diego had given him.

Paolo got back in the car and started the engine.

"Are these real?" I held up the passport. The photo was the same one I had taken for my university ID a week ago.

"Yes," was all he responded. I couldn't begin to imagine what sort of power a person had to have to get a genuine passport with a phony identity—in a week.

"Julie? Julie Jones?" That was the name they'd given me. "Not very creative, are you?"

He shrugged. "It's a name people easily forget."

"Is this really happening?" I said to myself.

We pulled back onto Highway 10, heading east. The morning sun had long ago transitioned into a bright, sunny afternoon. "Give it time. You'll adjust," he said.

"How many times have you done this? I mean, taken someone into hiding."

"A few," he replied.

"Oh." In a million years, I could never have imagined this was his life. "So why did you come back? I mean, my father could've assigned someone else to babysit me at college."

Paolo shrugged. "I took you on again because he asked. I'm his best."

Arrogant much? "So you didn't want to come back?"

"No." He glanced at me, with no sign of apology in his eyes.

"Don't blame you, I guess. Watching the boss's daughter can't be very exciting."

"I wouldn't say that," he replied, and a smile twitched across his lips.

"Then why didn't you want to be assigned to me?"

"I have my reasons," he replied.

"A man of few words."

"Yes." He smiled.

Oh, now I knew he was teasing. "Stop that."

"Okay."

I slapped his arm. "I mean it."

"Ow." He feigned being hurt and rubbed the spot. A few moments of silence passed, and I watched as his eyes focused on the road while his jaw muscles worked, giving away the wheels turning in his head. "I didn't want to be assigned to you, because I am very attracted to you," he finally said. He didn't look at me, and I was glad. He'd only see me trying to hide a smile.

"Is that why you left?" I asked.

"Your father is one of the most powerful men in the world. He would not appreciate me...*appreciating* his daughter." I felt a shameless, and admittedly shallow, little glow inside my chest. He considered me a temptation.

"Who does he work for?" I asked.

"For no one. That's what makes him powerful. That, and no one knows who he is, except me and a few of his most-trusted men."

The way Paolo described him, my father sounded like a mob boss.

"Can you at least tell me if he works for the good guys?" I asked.

"Good is a slightly subjective term—survival of the fittest might be more appropriate. But his customers, so to speak, are the obvious players."

I assumed he meant the U.S. government or their allies, but it still didn't sit well with me knowing he and his men were a bunch of international 007s.

"So that photo of you I found on the Internet—why was it there if you're a spy?" I asked.

"I'm not a spy."

"Do you kill people?"

"I have, but that's not my primary function. I'm not a hit man," he explained.

Right. How had he explained it before? "You just gather information and get paid not to exist. So, you're a ghost with a curious streak?"

He smirked. "You could say that."

"Except your picture is on the Internet."

"Not anymore. We killed that site after that little incident with you. But it *was* one of the ways we communicated without contacting each other. Your father had posted it so I'd send him a flare."

"Flare?"

"It's a signal to—never mind. The less you know, the better. It's too dangerous."

So I'd nabbed this "ghost's" photo off the Internet and used it to build my fake boyfriend. "Wrong place at the wrong time. Poor you."

"What do you mean?" he asked.

"That if I'd picked someone else's picture, you wouldn't be here right now."

He shrugged. "Must have been fate. Your father already had a few people assigned to you and was in the process of finding you someone more permanent for college. Male. He'd already approached me, but I'd turned him down." Paolo looked at me. "For obvious reasons."

Was he referring to finding me attractive?

"Well," I said. "It's nice to know, I suppose, that my dad *tries* to take care of me."

Paolo glanced at me. "He loves you. He's always put your safety first, assigned his best people to you and your mother."

Best people. Like who? Christ. "Mandy? She's one of the other..." I didn't know what to call them if they weren't spies. "People?"

"Don't be silly," he replied. "She couldn't find her way out of a paper bag."

"Hey! She's my best friend." I supposed it didn't make sense that she'd be one of them. After all, I'd known her

160

since elementary school. "Are you going to tell me who then?"

"No. But they all moved on after Janice hit you. They failed to do their job."

Had he meant the people were fired? I sank down in my seat and let the craziness in my head settle. "But Janice wasn't some spy, was she?"

"No. Janice was a complete fluke—I checked it out myself. She just went crazy."

From where I sat, crazy was not such a foreign concept. "I thought I'd imagined you, you know. I thought I was losing my mind."

"I'm sorry, but it hadn't gone as planned. Your father was supposed to fill you in before I arrived, but then you were hit by that truck, and he got called away to an emergency at the same time. I was under strict orders not to tell you anything."

"So you just let me believe I was insane and used intimidation to keep me in line?" I said.

"I didn't have a choice. And as long as I kept you safe, I knew we'd sort the rest out later. Once your father resurfaced, we did. More or less. Your father pulled me off and assigned someone else to you."

"Why?" I asked.

Paolo shrugged but didn't reply. Maybe he simply wanted to save me from hearing something unpleasant, such as I was a complete pain in his ass.

"Who took your place?" I asked drearily.

"I can't discuss the details."

My mind wouldn't let that one go, of course. I started to sift through the faces at school. Had there been anyone new my senior year who'd arrived after Santiago disappeared?

"Oh my God! Pierre? The French exchange student?" I asked.

Paolo didn't respond.

"I kept wondering why anyone would show up so late in the year. And I bumped into that guy everywhere. Mandy said he was following me."

Of course, I hadn't cared. I'd been so messed up after Santiago—Paolo left that nothing seemed to matter, not even my raging popularity. I'd tried dating a couple of times, wanting to forget. Even went out with Dax once, but when he'd kissed me there was no spark. Nothing. All I could think of was Santiag—*Christ*—Paolo. *It's going to take me forever to get used to his real name.*

"You're name *is* Paolo, right?" I asked. "Because I'm not going through the effort of learning a new name only to find out later on that you're Bob or Mike or Buford."

"Buford? If that were my real name, I'd change it anyway."

"Good point."

"My real name is Paolo," he confirmed.

Paolo. Italian for Paul. I chewed on that for a moment. I supposed he looked like a Paolo, but I was still trying to grasp him not being the sexy Spaniard Santiago.

"How old are you?"

"Just turned twenty-three."

Well, at least that wasn't a surprise. "How long have you been working for my dad?"

"I met your father when I was nineteen, but started working for him when I was twenty. Next question?"

"What's your last name?"

"I prefer not to say," he replied. "What you don't know can't hurt you."

"Why would knowing that hurt me?"

"If you're ever…captured." He spat out the last word like a curse. "I have family to protect, too."

"Oh." Captured. Because my father was some very powerful man who probably had tons of enemies just itching to find a crack in his armor.

Paolo must have noticed the horror on my face because he reached over and put his hand on my thigh. "Nothing's going to happen."

I expected him to remove his hand, but instead he left it there. Did he realize what he was doing to me? The gesture wasn't nearly as intimate as what we'd done last night, but it

162

somehow felt like it. I stared at his large, powerful hand for what seemed like an eternity, remembering how he'd touched my breasts and hips, remembering how he'd taken his hard, hot flesh and rubbed it against me through his jeans.

My stomach began to flutter wildly and my nipples tingled into sharp little points like giant lighthouses, signaling that I wanted him now just as much as I'd wanted him last night.

Shit. What am I thinking? I moved my leg away and turned my head toward the window, closing my eyes.

I didn't know why he wanted to touch me, since he'd made it clear we could never cross that line he'd drawn. But then he promptly removed his hand.

Breathe, Dakota. Just breathe. I wanted him to put the hand back immediately. It felt comforting, and I was beginning to realize that my feelings were much more than simple lust. I was falling in love with my ghost.

CHAPTER TWENTY-THREE

Just after sunset, Paolo pulled into a small motel away from the main highway on the east side of Las Cruces, New Mexico. We'd made a quick stop for supplies, picking up toiletries, sandwiches, clothes, and a backpack for me. It had been the fastest Target shopping trip of my life because I was simply too tired to care about what Paolo might think of me wearing sweats, which is what I bought. Three sets. Lord, how far I'd sunk in fashion. They weren't even cool, vintage-looking sweats, like those fun 1970s-style Puma jogging suits. And given where things had ended up between Paolo and me—not the steamy, hot place I pined for—I'd grabbed a couple sports bras and those really super-comfy panties in the multipack. I'd be damned if I'd be on the run, picking a thong out of my ass—not even to appease my ego.

"You shower first," he said, "while I set this stuff up." He plunked a large duffel bag on the motel room table.

"Thanks." I grabbed my shopping bag, relieved to have a few moments to myself and to get out of my grubby, dirty clothes. I turned on the hot shower and let it wash away the film of sweat and smoke stuck to my skin, trying not to think about what would happen to my life. I scrubbed and scrubbed until my skin felt clean and new, but the worries only made me feel heavy, tired. Sadly, there was no one to really turn to. Paolo had made it clear that I was…his work. And if he truly had lost the woman he once loved because he'd gotten too close, well, what could I say? I'd keep a distance from me, too.

I dressed in the bathroom, blow-dried my hair, and brushed my teeth to a pristine shine. When I finally came out, Paolo was staring at me like he'd just seen an alien.

"What?" I asked.

"One hour. How is it humanly possible to shower for one entire hour?"

"I was dirty?"

He smiled. "Well, I'm pleased to see you have skin left." He glanced at the table, which had a laptop connected to several cell phones and a small black box. "Don't touch that, got it?"

"But what if ET comes by and wants to call his mother?" I asked.

"Tell him to fuck off."

"Noted. But what is all that stuff?" I asked.

He scratched his whiskered chin. "Well, that," he pointed to the black box, "is a kind of phone hacker device. If I have someone's cell phone signature, I can program my phone to tell me what calls they make and receive, or even block them from calling certain numbers."

Grrr... "Like the police, for example?" I remembered my call being blocked in San Diego after I'd booted Paolo from my car. Then there was the time back at my house when I couldn't call anyone except my parents.

"Maaaybe." He flashed a mischievous grin. "But right now I'm using it to scramble my signal. Only data can get through, so the cell tower thinks it's a WiFi device like a portable GPS or an iPad, but not a phone. It makes it harder for anyone to trace—if they're trying to find us via a cell signal."

"Can I e-mail my mom?"

He shook his head. "I said 'harder,' not impossible. And we definitely don't know who's watching your mom's e-mail." He looked at his watch. "Just don't touch. I'll be right back."

Paolo disappeared into the bath, and I plunked down on the bed, resting my back against the headboard. My notebook was on the nightstand next to the remote for the TV. *How sweet.* Santiago—*ugh*—Paolo must have put it there for me. I opened it up and found my favorite beautiful pen inside.

I skimmed the leather binding and admired the beautiful thick paper of the pages. It was almost a shame to write it in, but once I started, I couldn't stop. Everything about the prior week came pouring out—my first days at school, thinking I'd lost my mind when I saw Paolo, realizing he was real, and knowing that there'd be no chance in hell of my forgetting him. I wrote about how looking at him made me feel, how his body felt next to mine, how he made me feel safe even though my world was falling apart. Before I knew it, tears streamed down my face. The stress and heavy emotions I'd been carrying around, including the anger I had for my father who'd hid so much of himself from me, exploded from the confines of that invisible space inside my head where all dark thoughts resided. I didn't even know who my father really was. And my mother? How could she have hidden all this from me?

"Dakota?" Paolo stood there staring at me, wearing faded button flies, a white towel slung over one shoulder, his shirtless chest expanding and contracting rapidly.

"What?" I wiped away my tears with the back of my hand.

"I heard you crying. I thought…" He sat down on the edge of the bed and stared at the floor for a moment before looking at me again with his hypnotic, deep brown eyes. I noticed then, as the light of the lamp on the nightstand illuminated his eyes, that they had flecks of bright gold around the irises. So beautiful. Just like the rest of him. His smooth olive skin, his thick arms and ripped stomach, everything about him was so addictive, so masculine.

He suddenly leaned over and kissed me. It was a soft kiss, at first. The kind a man might give a woman to comfort her when he's unable to say how he feels. But what did I know? I'd never been with anyone. Nor did I truly ever want to be unless it was Paolo, which is why it was impossible for me not to react to his touch, to his hand moving to my cheek, to the smell of his clean skin flooding my nostrils.

The kiss suddenly became *me* trying to communicate the words I couldn't say…*I want you. I need you.* But it would be silly to need someone so much when I didn't really know him, wouldn't it? So why did I feel that way?

His tongue slid into my mouth, and I savored the feeling of him inside me. No, it wasn't sex, but it was the closest we'd ever get. His hand moved to the back of my hair and pulled me closer, deepening the kiss. The way he tried to mold me to him, to make me fit against his male frame, overwhelmed my senses.

I moved my hand to his chest and let it glide over the rounded, firm contours of his muscles. As we sat there facing each other, letting our lips and tongues do the talking, my mind dipped a toe in the water. If I told him I really wanted him, really wanted to make him my first, what would he say? Another rejection? I didn't have the strength to endure another one of those. Not now.

But when his hand moved from the back of my neck to my shoulder and gently pushed me into the bed, I felt the simultaneous explosion of relief and the flood of sensual heat throughout my body. I don't know if he sensed the reaction, but the pace of his kiss turned frantic, and I followed along eagerly.

He stretched out against the length of my body and slid his leg between mine. I instantly felt the thickness of his erection pressing into my hip bone, making the spark between my thighs turn into a throbbing ache that blazed through my core.

His hand slid up my sweatshirt and cupped my breast. "God, I love your body, Dakota," he panted in between frantic hard kisses.

I turned toward him and slid my hand into the waistband of his jean, wanting to explore the soft skin and hard muscle of his ass. It felt even better than it looked.

I pulled him into me, signaling with my body how much I desired him, but he held back.

He slowed the kiss and looked at me. "Do you really want to do this?" he asked.

"Yes." I touched the side of his stubbled face, hoping he'd see the tension screaming inside my body. "But do you?"

He stared for a moment. "You know I can't give you anything. No relationship. No phone number. Nothing."

It sucked, but I knew. And maybe a small part of me believed if given the chance, he'd change his mind. Just like I'd changed mine about him. "I don't care."

He kissed me hard, and that's when I felt him let go. He wasn't trying to be careful and kind or protect me; he was simply a guy giving into his needs, his desire. For me.

He lifted up my sweatshirt and his lips worked their way down until they found my nipple. He licked it slowly and then kissed every inch of my breast. "You have the most beautiful tits I've ever seen."

That was really nice, but…"Paolo, please. You don't need to warm me up."

He lifted a brow and smiled. He went to his knees and began removing my sweatpants. "Wow. I did not see those coming."

I looked down at my neon orange Fruit of the Loom bikini briefs. "What? I needed comfort. It's been a hard day."

"No, I think they are very…hot." He grinned.

I laughed as he began kissing me at the waist and sliding down my "man killers," leaving me exposed. He stared at my most intimate domain for a moment. "Damn it, Dakota. Is there any part of you that's not perfect?"

He dipped his head and kissed me just over my throbbing, tingling bud, then slid his tongue inside, finding the tender, hot flesh. I grabbed fistfuls of sheets, having never felt anything so erotic, so sinful.

"You taste even better," he whispered.

Oh my God, if he doesn't get on with this, I'm going to cross the finish line without him. "Paolo, please. Please don't do any more. I am ready. Really, really ready."

"Patience, Dakota. It's your first time. It should be memorable."

Yeah. Little did he know that memorable was in the eye of the beholder. That scratchy tree trunk from last night would have been hunky-dory with me. Just as long as I was with him.

"I could never, ever forget you," I panted.

He looked up at me and tilted his head in a strange way, and I wondered why. He crawled up my body and hovered over my face. "I'm going to fuck you so hard that you won't even remember your name."

I swallowed. "Ummm…Okay." The words came out scratchy and dry.

He kneeled between my legs and began sliding down his pants. His thick erection sprang from his pants, savage and hungry. I was just about to ask about protection, praying he had something in his wallet, when the phone on the desk vibrated loudly on top of the laminated surface.

We both jumped. "Hell. That's your father," he grumbled.

What? "My father?" I scrambled away from Paolo, horrified by some irrational fear that he knew what Paolo and I were doing at that very moment.

How idiotic! I was a grown woman with nothing to be ashamed of.

I shook my head while Paolo arranged himself, took a breath, and then sat down at his laptop. He logged in and read.

His back was to me, so I couldn't see his face, but his sagging posture radiated defeat, disappointment, and possibly something much, much worse.

"What? What is it?" I asked.

He didn't reply. I got up from the bed and slid on my panties. "What? What did he write?" I demanded.

His head drooped. "I am to hand you over to someone else tomorrow morning."

"But why?" I asked.

He rubbed his forehead. "I don't know."

"Well, answer him back. Tell him no."

Paolo didn't turn around or look at me. "I can't."

"Can't or won't?" I asked.

"Both, and you know why," he said quietly.

Yeah. I knew…he didn't want to fight for me. Whatever hold the past had over him was stronger than anything he felt for me. I guess he had his own ghost to deal with. "Sure."

I flipped off the lamp and got under the covers, turning my back to him.

"Dakota, this is my job. If your father is asking me to hand you off, it's for a damned good reason. He depends on me to follow orders. That's the deal."

I closed my eyes and silently berated myself. I'd known this was "the deal," but that didn't make it any easier watching him choose his job and his ghost over me.

Paolo lay down behind me and wrapped his arms around my waist, nuzzling his rough cheek into the back of my neck. "I wish things were different."

Me, too…

ॐ

The next morning, Paolo packed up his equipment while I showered yet again. I wanted to see him as little as possible before being delivered like a prisoner to a new penitentiary. I pulled my hair back into a neat bun and stared myself down in the mirror. *You will not cry, you will not cry. Do you hear me, Dakota Dane? You will not…*

Oh shit. I'm so going to cry.

Well, to hell with it.

I emerged from the bathroom avoiding eye contact with Paolo.

"Ready?" he asked.

"Sure." I threw my stuff in my backpack and marched to the truck, holding my chin up high.

The moment he got behind the wheel, he took a deep breath, looked at me with his mouth halfway open, and then pressed his lips together. Whatever he wanted to say, he'd changed his mind. Good. Because no words could make me feel better. I simply couldn't understand how he could do this.

We drove through town in silence, and when we pulled into the police station my nerves took over.

"Why here?" I asked, thinking we'd do the exchange in the back of some seedy bar.

"It's safer. Lots of witnesses. Not to mention, I have friends here."

I remembered Paolo's "friend" at the San Diego PD. "And just why is that? Aren't you people supposed to be ghosts who don't exist?"

He thought about his answer. "Even ghosts need friends, but they don't know what I do or who I am. They only know they get paid well for keeping an eye on things for me from time to time, and I pass them helpful information when it comes my way."

"So what did your 'friend' give you the night I saw you outside the police station in San Diego?" I asked.

"I had your new identity package sent there for safekeeping. But in addition to that? He gave me information about your roommate and everyone in your classes."

"So you check out every single person who comes into contact with me?" I asked.

"Pretty much. Thank God you're antisocial. It's a lot of fucking work."

Ass.

A white SUV pulled into an empty spot a few cars down. "Wait here," he ordered.

I watched the other driver, a bald man with a cold stare, exit his vehicle and greet Paolo with a handshake. I sincerely hoped Paolo had done his homework on this guy; he looked scarier than shit.

They started talking and Paolo waved me over.

My entire body surged with adrenaline and pulsed with anger as I approached the man. How could Paolo leave me with some creepy stranger when my life was a horrible nightmare? This couldn't be real. This couldn't be happening. But the man's icy, blue eyes instantly zeroed in on me, extinguishing my rage with a cold chill.

"Dakota," he nodded his head. "Nice to meet you. Your father speaks very highly of you."

"Dakota," Paolo said, "this is Derek. He'll be watching over you."

I looked at Paolo. "For how long?" My insides were trembling. Something didn't feel right.

"As long as it takes," Derek replied.

I whispered to Paolo, "Please, I'm begging you. Don't do this. I don't know him."

Paolo gripped my shoulders. "You'll be fine," he said, without a flicker of emotion in his tone.

"I don't want to go with him. I don't care what my father told you. Please, Paolo! Please!"

His eyes dropped for a moment and then hardened. "You can't stay with me. So you'll go with him, or you'll be alone. Those are your choices."

So that was it. Everything we'd been through. Everything we felt—well, perhaps that was my fatal flaw. He felt lust; I felt more. He warned me not to. I didn't listen. *The sucker gets what the sucker deserves.*

I lifted my chin. "Thank you, Derek. I'll try to make your *job* as easy as possible." I looked at Paolo. "I'm a piece of cake; *easiest* job you've ever had. Right?"

After all, I was just some sex kitten ready to pounce on his yarn any chance I got. Can't get any easier.

Irritation flickered in his eyes. "You were great."

"See. Nothing to worry about, Derek," I said. "Good-bye, Paolo."

I loaded myself into the white SUV.

Don't look back, don't look back, I commanded myself as we pulled out of the lot. I felt Paolo's eyes following our truck from across the lot. Unable to resist, I looked back and saw the expression of a man who didn't care.

Why did I look back?

So you remember not to cry over him. He doesn't care about you.

Easier said than done, but I was determined not to. I would bury any feelings I had for the man and shove them down a deep, dark hole. I would not crumble. I would not shed one tear for a guy who didn't care about me.

࿐

For the first thirty miles or so, Derek didn't say much other than a few yeses and nos. He was more robotic than Paolo had ever been, which made me extremely uncomfortable. But then again, the entire situation felt uncomfortable.

"Where are we going?" I asked. I knew Paolo had intended to take me somewhere in Texas, given the direction we'd been heading and the fact he'd said it would be a two-day drive. But Derek had gotten onto Highway 25, north toward Albuquerque.

"A safe house, a few hours from here," he replied.

Paolo had said it was the first thing *he* did: establish a level one safe house. And he made it clear that no one else would know its whereabouts, so it made sense that Derek would take me somewhere different.

"I guess my dad didn't give you a lot of time to prepare," I said.

"Prepare what?" he asked.

"The safe house."

"We have people who take care of all that," he replied.

Shit. He was lying. Paolo had specifically said that they never trusted anyone with that work.

Maybe you misheard Paolo. Maybe he'd said only he *did all his own safe house prep?*

Ask another question.

"Thank goodness," I said. "I can only imagine how busy you guys get with all of your spying and killing people. My dad says he can't keep up half the time."

The guy bobbed his head. "Yeah. Well, comes with the territory."

173

Holy crap. Paolo had been very, very clear; my dad's people were not spies or assassins. They were very skilled information gatherers. Yes, that sounded like a spy to me, but he saw a distinct difference. In any case, whoever this guy was, I was pretty sure he wasn't on my dad's team. What was I going to do?

Think, think, think…

"Derek, I'm so sorry, but I've really got to use the bathroom. I drank way too much coffee this morning. Can we stop? I think I saw a sign for a gas station at the next exit."

"We need more road behind us first. You'll have to wait."

Don't panic. Don't panic…"I really can't. Have the bladder of an acorn. It's really annoying."

He glanced at me with those cold, blue eyes. "Sure. No problem." From the corner of my eye, I saw him reach into his pocket and slam something into my leg. The needle stuck out like a porcupine quill, and whatever he gave me was potent. My hand didn't even make it to my thigh to pull it out.

I am so screwed.

CHAPTER TWENTY-FOUR

Time is one of those funny things. When you're busy enjoying life, it seems to pass by so quickly that hours can feel like minutes. And when you're terrified, waiting for the inevitable, minutes can feel like days. I don't know how long I was unconscious, but when I woke up on the floor in the windowless room with a single lightbulb dangling from the ceiling, the dankness in the air telling me I was likely in some basement, well, the minutes felt like weeks.

Paolo had said that if my father's enemies ever got a hold of me, they'd remove my head and ship it off in a box. Every breath I took, every beat of my heart would be my last, I thought. I may never see my mother again and have the chance to hug her. I may never see my father or Paolo again either, which meant I may never get to kick them in their man baskets.

Frigging men! This was all their fault.

Well, culpability aside, I needed to get myself out of this, starting with a way to defend myself. I slowly got up and looked around for something—anything—for defense, but there was nothing in the room except a mattress on the cold cement floor, a small, doorless bathroom with only a toilet— no lid on the tank—and a sink. Nothing else. If I were strong enough, I could throw the toilet at my captors, but sprouting Hulk-like powers wasn't going to happen to me.

Hopeless.

And hopelessness only turned into utter despair as I thought through the events that led me to this place. Paolo had handed me over to go into hiding. He'd said that in my case, when there was a leak, all communication would be broken. Possibly for months.

He wouldn't know I'd been taken.

No one would come looking for me.

I was a dead woman.

The door opened, startling me from my deep, dark thoughts. When I looked, however, it wasn't Derek, but a very familiar face. "Mr. M?"

"Dakota."

I was about ready to run over to him and hug him, but one obvious question prevented me from doing that. "What the hell?"

He pointed toward the mattress. "Please, sit."

"Not until you tell me what the fuck is going on."

"Sit!" he screamed. That's when I noticed the wild, desperate look in his eyes bloodshot eyes.

I was already past the point of terrified, so his screaming didn't intimidate me exactly, but I did want to hear what he had to say. Simply put...why the hell was my English teacher holding me hostage in a basement?

I sat cross-legged on the mattress and waited for him to speak. Mr. M paced across the cement floor, mumbling frantically and running his hand over his thinning hair. Usually, his clothes were a wrinkled mess, but now he looked worse, like he'd been sleeping in them for a week. Then he began to do a disturbing little dance, wiggling his hips, making the number one sign with his index fingers.

I simply stared, unable to believe my eyes.

He twirled on his heel and pointed. "Gotcha! I got her! The best-hid girl in the world, and I," he pointed to himself, "got her! With a fucking pen! Ha! Take that, Mr. Dane!"

With a pen? My pen? I suddenly remembered what Paolo had said about tracking devices. It was the reason he hadn't wanted me to take anything personal from my dorm.

Mr. M laughed like a madman, the veins popping from his forehead as he did. "I'm not going to lie to you, Dakota, you are going to die. The only question is how."

Holy shit. Not good. "And I've done what, exactly, to deserve this?" I asked.

"You've done nothing. Nothing. But that bastard father of yours ruined my life, so now I'm going to ruin his. I'm going to make it hurt while I do it."

"If you plan on torturing me," I said quietly, "I can save you the trouble. I only just learned who my father is, and other than knowing he's some high-powered information broker, I barely know the man."

He laughed again, howling at the ceiling. "Is that what he told you? Your evil bastard of a father is much, much more than a librarian. The CIA and Interpol are his lapdog whores! He's the man behind the curtain," Mr. M waved his red, sweaty palms through the air like a magician at a border town carnival, "who decides who lives or dies."

"But he's the g…g…good guy," I mumbled.

"Is he? Is he *good*? Because I worked for him for years, my *dear Dakota*, and there are a few hundred thousand people who've died who might not agree. He's a ruthless, fucking animal."

I couldn't believe that.

Okay, okay. I didn't exactly know the man, but he wasn't psycho. He worked hard, loved me and my mom, and tried to keep us away from whatever crap he was mixed up in.

Yeah. And has a secret life—an army at his beck and call, including the police, and people who are scared shitless of him. But "fucking animal"?

Crap. Had that been the real reason Paolo resisted getting involved with me?

My jaw dropped. Paolo said that my father would kill him for touching me. I assumed he'd meant it figuratively, but perhaps not. Add the fact that my father had some very determined enemies, and, well, maybe he wasn't such a good guy.

"Then why did you work for him?" I asked.

"He's the lesser of evils. But a good guy? Not a fucking chance, my dear Miss Dane. And his luck just caught up with him."

I swallowed hard, wondering what they would do to me. Then I remembered poor Christy. I now had to assume the fire had been meant for me. "So what's next? Are you going to burn me alive like you did that poor girl?" They'd probably videotape it for my parents, or something sick like that.

"That little fire was just to get you on the run, away from your other guards so we could easily take you."

Other guards? Why was I surprised?

"I plan to sell your body." Mr. M shook his head, and beads of sweat streamed down from his temples.

"How can you do this? I thought you cared about me." I'd seemed to be making that mistake a lot.

"Your father fired me after that little bitch Janice ran you over. I spent my entire life in his service! And just like *that*," he snapped his fingers, "he turned me out. I lost everything!" Mr. M screamed. "Because I don't fucking exist in the real world! I can't get a normal job."

"So you're going to get even by killing me? How will that solve anything?" I asked.

He shook his finger in the air. "Ah! It won't. But selling you to the highest bidder will. There are people who'll pay millions just for the pleasure of sending your body, piece by piece, to your father."

If I ever got free, I made a mental note to ask my father, *What the fuck?* I wasn't sure I believed he was the spawn of Satan; however, he had to be doing a lot more than simply gathering information and protecting a few people if his enemies were willing to pay millions for the joy of chopping me up.

Christ. What a bunch of sick, evil bastards. No wonder Paolo was paranoid.

Now, so was I.

"If it's any consolation," I said, "I thought you were the best teacher I'd ever had. I cried when you retired—wasn't even sure how I'd get through the rest of my senior year without you."

Anger flickered in his eyes. "Then you know a fraction of the pain your father has caused me."

He left the room and promptly returned, tossing my backpack on the floor. "Get comfortable, it will be a few days before we find a buyer." He left, and I heard him bolt the door.

I stared at the floor for what seemed like an hour. Maybe two. A little over five months ago I was just about to turn eighteen, sitting in Mr. M's homeroom, pining for a cute boy, and wishing my life would change. I was a girl—naive, awkward, lonely. A few months had changed all that.

I grabbed my backpack and riffled through it. My clothes were still there along with my toothbrush—*Oh goody. Wouldn't want my teeth to be dirty when they are shipped off in that nice* FedEx *box*—and my notebook. The frigging pen was still in there.

I unscrewed the top and shook out its contents. There was the inkwell attached to the ballpoint, and inside the cap was a tiny little wire, about the length of a grain of rice. I chucked it into the toilet. "Asshole."

I reassembled the pen and opened up my book. I wrote about how Paolo had unknowingly handed me over to my father's enemies, who drugged me and took me to some horrible dark basement. I wrote about how Mr. M was behind it all and crazy as a loon, seeking money and revenge.

But sitting here alone, I wrote, *in this dingy basement, knowing that in a few days I'll be sold to the highest bidder, I still can't bring myself to be mad at Paolo for this when he only did what he thought was best. He thought he was saving me. If anyone ever finds this—if you, Paolo, ever find this, please know that I don't blame you. In some twisted way, I find myself appreciating you even more. Your fatal flaw is loyalty. Perhaps, even, devotion. Both are things I'd always hoped to find in the man I'd love forever. But I guess it just wasn't meant to be. My only regret is that I never had the chance to tell you that I think our ghosts, our fears from the past aren't there to hold us back or to make us feel afraid, but to teach us to value what we have. To fight for what we love. Losing everything has taught me that.*

I love you. And if you find this, I want you to know that I will haunt you, but only so you'll remember not to let the next woman slide through your fingers.

"Damn it. I'm so corny!" Was this really what I wanted to leave behind?

I scribbled wildly over my words, blacking out every letter.

Dear Paolo and Dad,

If you find this. Give those bastards hell and make them pay.

Love,
Dakota

P.S. Mom, I love you.

I sighed with contentment. That felt much better. If the world was full of sick, evil people who enjoyed kidnapping and dissecting the innocent, well, I was damned glad there were men out there ready to take them down.

CHAPTER TWENTY-FIVE

Two days later…

"Get up."

Cold water splashed on my face, bringing me out of my deep sleep. Mr. M stood over me, holding an empty glass.

"Thanks," I grumbled, and wiped my damp eyes.

"You're welcome. Now, go do what you need to do; we have a long drive."

I stood up and looked at Mr. M. He still wore the same filthy clothes after two full days.

"How much did they offer?" I asked. If I was going to die, I wanted to know what my sad little life was worth.

"Three million," he replied. "Two million nine hundred ninety-nine thousand dollars too much."

"Thanks," I said. "You're a scrumptious, charming man."

"I'll give you two minutes," he said with disdain, giving me a little privacy to wash up and pee.

Two minutes on the nose, he was back. He dragged me up the creaky, dark stairs, through the dilapidated ranch-style house and outside toward a green sedan parked on a long gravel driveway. The surrounding trees and cactus garden hinted that we were still in New Mexico or Arizona, but I didn't know for sure.

As we approached the car, he told me to put my hands behind my back.

"Going to drug me again?" I asked.

"I'm going to handcuff you. I want you awake for your new owners; they plan to send lots and lots of videos to your father before killing you."

I winced. "Nice, Mr. M. Really, really nice."

He frowned. "Turn."

I did as he asked. After all, what was the point in fighting him when he might change his mind and stick me with another needle, leaving me completely helpless? This way, I might see an opportunity for escape and be awake to take it.

He opened the back passenger side door and shoved me inside before moving to the driver's seat. Derek was nowhere to be found. "Where is your friend?" I asked.

"He's gone on ahead to secure—"

Blood exploded over the interior of the car and my face. I screamed. A chunk of Mr. M's head was gone, and his body bucked violently as what I assumed was another silent bullet hit him in the chest. Then another.

My door flew open, and a man in a black ski mask dragged me from the car. I screamed again and tried to fight, but my hands were tied back.

"Shit, Dakota. Calm down. It's me."

"Paolo?"

The man removed his mask. "Yes." He looked over his shoulder. "We need to get the fuck out of here."

I'd never been so relieved in my life. And so terrified.

Paolo dragged me across a small field at the right of the house and through a standing of trees to where a motorcycle waited. Panting, he asked me to turn around. He freed my hands and then took off his black jacket and removed his shirt. "Clean your face with this."

I wiped away what I could and threw the shirt on the ground before he popped a helmet on my head. "Just hang on." He put his jacket back on and started the engine.

I jumped on behind him, wrapping my arms around his waist and basking in the comfort of feeling safe, of being with him. I wasn't letting go this time.

☙☞

Taking only back roads, Paolo didn't stop for hours. He could have kept driving forever for all I cared. Just as long as I was away from that place and those men. I didn't care that my face was still smudged with Mr. M's blood or that my back and arms were numb from being on that bike and squeezing Paolo as if he were my lifeline to sanity.

When he finally pulled off at a small gas station near the Oasis State Park in New Mexico, he had to pry my hands off him. "Dakota, it's okay now." He removed his helmet and looked at me with his dark eyes. "You're all right."

How could he be so calm and collected?

"Nod if you understand me," he said.

I nodded.

"That's my girl."

My girl. My girl. My hands balled into fists.

He must've seen the rage in my eyes because his expression hardened.

"Don't," he warned. "Not here. I know you're angry and traumatized, but you need to hold it together, all right? Just until we're somewhere safe, and then, I promise, you can scream at me all you like."

I didn't respond.

"Please, Dakota?"

I nodded.

"Good. There's a bathroom. Go inside and wash up. I'll get you something to drink. Are you hungry, too?"

"No," I murmured.

He ran his hand down my arm. "I know how you feel."

How could he possibly know how I felt? I dismounted from the bike and walked to the exterior entrance of the bathroom, keeping my helmet on. When I locked the door, I removed it and looked at my face in the foggy, scuffed up mirror. I didn't recognize myself. I looked like a creature from a horror movie. Chunks of dried blood were matted in my hair and stuck to my brows. I washed and scrubbed, but I still felt dirty. The image of Mr. M's head exploding kept replaying in my mind. I rinsed my mouth with soap several times, remembering how some of his blood got inside it. I'd never forget that taste. The taste of death and salvation. And terror.

"No. You're not doing this, Dakota. He got what he deserved. You're alive. That's all that matters," I told myself, and sucked back the raw emotions.

There wasn't much I could do about the blood on my shirt, so I finished drying my face and met Paolo outside.

When his eyes met mine, the air left my lungs. He was so beautiful, a vision of fierce masculinity, standing there next to his bike. But that look…Something in his dark eyes gripped me deep inside and threatened to unravel the shred of sanity I clung to. Was it rage I saw? Or love? Perhaps both? Maybe it was the look of a man who simply wanted revenge.

"I bought this for you inside. Put it on." He handed me a sweatshirt with a giant saguaro cactus on the front. It looked like a green pickle, and if we were in any other situation, I might have laughed. But we weren't, so I didn't. I slipped it on, and he handed me a Gatorade, which I chugged.

"Better?" he asked.

"Better," was all I managed to say.

He put his hand on my face. His dark eyes still carried that look of turmoil. "Never again."

He turned away and got on the bike. I got behind him.

Never again what?

CHAPTER TWENTY-SIX

We drove for six more hours, a blur of cactus, gas stations, dirt, and road signs, until we reached a town called Lago Vista in Texas, somewhere North of Austin from what I gathered from the signs. The sun had already retreated, and I was shivering to the bone, though it really wasn't cold outside. The autumn air was actually balmy and tropical.

Paolo pulled up to a modern, two-story, white house surrounded by trees and perched on a small hill at the edge of a large lake.

I looked around at the other homes off in the distance. "Is *this* the safe house?" I asked. I had imagined another rustic cabin hidden in the woods, or a broken-down old ranch house like the one where I'd been held captive.

He bobbed his head but didn't look at me. "Come on." He went to the side gate and reached over to pop it open. Although it was dark outside, the exterior was well lit, and I could see that the home was huge. I walked into the backyard and immediately noticed how the lights of the houses on the other side danced and sparkled in the early evening waves. I took a deep breath and savored the calmness. Paolo had taken me to the perfect place to lick my wounds and come to terms with what had just happened.

"Are you hungry?" Paolo's hands gently squeezed my shoulders from behind.

"No," I whispered. Food was the last thing on my mind.

"A bath then."

"It's beautiful," I said, still looking out across the hypnotic ripples. "Thank you."

"Come inside," he said dryly.

I followed quietly, and began to wonder what was going on in his head. Maybe he thought the angry girl from back at the gas station was about to make an appearance and give

185

him a bitter taste of her mind. But that girl was exhausted and unsure of what to do or how to feel.

The interior of the home was just as large and impressive as one might imagine. Everything—furniture, floors, and walls—were shades of white. Pristine. He led me upstairs and showed me the large master bedroom and bath. The steaming jet tub was already half filled.

"I had the service stock everything. There are toothbrushes and supplies in the cabinet. Extra towels and a robe are there, too. I can wash what you have and take you to buy clothes in the morning, but the robe will have to do for tonight." He shut the door behind him and left me standing in the enormous, bright bathroom. Alone.

I shut off the water and stared at the tub. I didn't want to soak. I didn't want to be alone. I wanted to get clean. I wanted answers.

My mind wouldn't stop spinning with questions, trying to work out the problems. I wanted to know why he'd let me go, and how the hell he'd found me. I wanted to know if I was truly safe now. I wanted to know where my father was and if my mother was okay.

Damn it. I've had it.

I came to the conclusion that their rules about not sharing information didn't apply to me anymore. I'd almost lost my life going along with "the deal." Their deal sucked, and it was time to push my way out of this godforsaken rabbit hole.

I quickly showered and cleaned myself up. I burst from the bathroom in a white robe, ready for that rant I'd been holding inside.

Paolo sat on the edge of the bed, wearing a plain white T-shirt and jeans, facing the bathroom door, like he'd been expecting this moment.

"How could you let me go?" I asked.

He didn't react or move; he simply stared with his cold, dark eyes.

"Answer me, goddamn it!" I screamed.

"You know why," he replied in a low, quiet voice, "and my saying it won't change anything."

"I'm not talking about the fact that you thought you were following orders. I'm talking about you letting me go when I begged you not to!"

"I know." His gaze was cold and distant, but I knew there was more going on inside that head of his, and I needed to know what it was.

"I want to hear you say it," I seethed.

"Say what?" he said in that deep, slow, thickly accented voice. "That I'm sorry? That I should've known? I don't need to waste my time stating the obvious."

"Not that. I want to hear you say it was a mistake to care more about that job of yours and pleasing my father than you did about me. I want to hear you promise you'll never do it again. That you understand some things are more important than following orders. Or are you too much of a coward? Too afraid to break the rules, even when it's the right thing to do? Huh? Tell me. I'd like to know."

He opened his mouth, but didn't say anything.

"I see," I said. "Then you get what you deserve. I just hope that hollow, dark hole you call a life doesn't swallow you up in your sleep."

He stood and walked over to me, that same look of turmoil I'd seen earlier percolating in the depths of his eyes. "It already did. The moment I let you go." He cupped my face with both hands. "I knew it was a mistake. Even before I found out it was a trap. But I let you go because I believed you were better off. I failed to keep my mother alive. I failed to keep my ex alive. I couldn't stop thinking you'd be next. And when I got the call from your father, telling me they'd taken you, I knew I was being punished for being such a coward, for being unable to let go of the past. I shouldn't have let you go."

He kissed me with desperation, holding me to his body. I didn't kiss him back. I don't know why. Maybe I was waiting for something to happen inside my chest. That warm, gooey, melting feeling that I'd experienced when he'd kissed me before. Instead, nothing happened. I felt numb and empty inside.

Sensing his kiss wasn't welcome, he pulled back and sighed. "Just know, I would have sold my soul to get you back."

"Bullshit! You were more pissed about being tricked. You and your badass ego couldn't stand knowing someone beat you. You're just like my father—can't stand to fail."

Paolo had a frustrated, wounded look on his face. "I didn't give a fuck about that. I wanted you back. That was the only thing that mattered."

I sat down on the bed and closed my eyes. I realized I was lashing out at him. "I need a moment."

"Take all the time you need. I'll be sleeping in the other room." He left with heavy footsteps.

Exhausted, I lay back on the bed. *Calm down. Calm down. You're safe now. You're safe…*But was I? Before, when I first met Paolo, I felt like my sanity was at stake. Then it evolved into a question of my physical well-being. Now, everything felt at risk. Mind, body, and soul. There wasn't one single piece left unscathed.

You can get through this, Dakota. You'll find a way.

I could only hope I was right.

I don't recall falling asleep, but when I heard Paolo scream, I landed on the floor.

Shit. I held my breath and listened, expecting to hear a struggle. There was nothing but an eerie silence blanketing the house.

I unplugged the lamp on the nightstand—a square, stainless steel thing with sharp corners—and tiptoed into the hallway. Paolo's bedroom door was wide open. With the orange glow of the clock on the nightstand, I saw him lying there in his boxer briefs, blankets and sheets tossed to the floor. He grumbled and twitched his arms.

I released a breath. He must've been having a nightmare.

I sat down next to him and looked at the troubled expression, creased brow and lids pushed tightly together.

"Paolo?" I whispered. "Paolo?" I shook him gently by the shoulder. "Wake up. You're having a bad dream."

His eyes flew open, and I found myself pinned beneath his large body, his fist raised in the air.

"It's me!" I screamed and turned my head to the side, expecting to get pummeled.

He froze. "Christ, Dakota. What are you doing?"

"I...I...heard you scream," I said.

"So you came to rescue me?"

"I guess."

He rolled off onto his back, panting. "Shit. I could've killed you."

"With your fist? No. But it would've hurt."

"There's a gun on the nightstand," he clarified. "You're lucky I didn't reach for it."

"Oh. Call me lucky then." We lay next to each other in silence, several moments passing. "What were you dreaming about?" I finally asked.

"You."

"Was I staring at your ass again?"

He laughed. "I wish."

"Then?"

"Your father called," he said.

"Did he threaten to kill you for touching me?" I asked.

"Yes. I mean, no. I mean, he really called."

"I thought we couldn't use a cell phone," I said, wondering about the safe house "no communication with the outside" rule.

"I'm sure he used precautions, but he needed me to know he'd be here in the morning to take you."

My heart sank. So this was the part where he'd let me go all over again.

"I quit," he added. "And I told him I love you."

His words repeated inside my head like an echo that didn't fade.

"You told him..." I swallowed. "You love me?"

Paolo's hand reached out and grabbed mine. "Yes. And he told me that if I lay a hand on you, he'd break me in two."

189

"But Paolo—"

"I told him he can go fuck himself. He'll have to pry you from my cold, dead hands."

Paolo wanted to fight for me. That was all I needed to hear. I rolled on top of him and kissed him with everything I had.

He pushed me back. "Dakota, I think we need to talk—"

"Now or never, Paolo. Decide. Because I'm not going to offer myself again."

"Now. Yes, now."

I kissed him hard and untied my robe, letting my naked body cover his. He groaned and rolled on top of me, settling himself between my thighs. I immediately felt his hot, hard flesh pressing against me. Every nerve ending in my body instantly pulsed with sensual waves of heat. It was nothing like before, when I'd simply wanted him to satisfy my lust. This came from another place, deep inside my soul. I wanted to lose myself in him and feel his body connect to mine.

Paolo slid his hand between us and stroked the heated fold between my legs. "God, Dakota. You're so wet, so hot." He dipped a finger inside, and I gasped. "I've never wanted anyone like I want you." He plunged another finger inside. "To make you come."

He covered my mouth with his, and continued stroking me with his hand, but that was not what I wanted.

I gently pushed his hand away. "You don't need to do that," I whispered in his ear.

Paolo eagerly took the cue and slid down his boxers. He reached over to the nightstand drawer, and I heard the swift deployment of a condom. I was grateful he'd had the house "stocked," but even more grateful when he returned his mouth to mine, continuing the frantic kiss. I felt him position his thick head at my entrance, and all I could think of was how incredibly whole I felt. Like a missing piece of my life had slipped into place, giving me the strength to face whatever would come next. I had Paolo. And I loved him.

He pushed inside me with one steady thrust, driving himself deep. I gasped from the pain, but the erotic pulsing tension, the need to release it, kept me from wanting him to stop.

His sensual assault repeated as he pulled out almost completely and thrust into me again, releasing a deep, masculine groan. Each time he did this, I felt a sharp delicious pain push my body to the brink of an explosion. But I didn't want it to end so quickly. I wanted it to last forever. His smooth olive skin and hard muscles working over my body, his thick muscular arms straining as he lifted his chest away so he could watch himself plunging inside me, his dark hair falling over his eyes as he watched me taking him in, it was better than I could have ever fantasized.

The sinful tension coiled tightly, and I knew my body was but a few hard strokes away from climaxing.

"Paolo," I panted.

"Come for me, Dakota." He pushed his hips sharply forward, driving the air from my lungs. He thrust once again. "I want to watch you." And again. "Come for me."

His raw, sexual words pushed me over the edge, and the walls seemed to crash down around me. My body exploded with every ounce of the pent-up heat I had for this gorgeous man as he came with one final, deep thrust. He groaned loudly in a sexy, animalistic sort of way that was so purely male it sparked goose bumps.

Several amazingly lucid moments passed where I felt like we were the only two people in existence, our pulses thrumming in unison.

"I love you," he said in a gravelly voice, and slowly began rocking into me, wringing out every last shudder.

"I love you, too," I finally whispered back after gaining my breath.

He dropped onto his elbows and kissed me with a slow, sated laziness. Once again, I don't remember falling asleep, but somehow in my dreams, I remember thinking that when I woke up, I'd be the happiest, sorest woman on the planet.

CHAPTER TWENTY-SEVEN

The unwelcome cell phone rang sometime during the early hours, ripping me away from the deepest sleep I'd had in months.

I cracked open an eye and stared at the thing. My exhausted mind didn't exactly register where I was, but the sound of Paolo's breath in my ear and the feel of his warm, naked body snuggled close to mine convinced me I was still dreaming.

I flopped my hand on top of the offending device and looked at the screen. "Who's four five seven?" I gently nudged Paolo with my elbow.

He grumbled and turned over, revealing his perfectly tanned, gorgeous, broad back. I looked down, and there it was. His ass.

It was quite possibly the nicest ass known to creation. Round and hard, the same deep olive skin as the rest of him. I sighed cheerfully and silenced the phone. Whoever was calling would have to wait. I snuggled my bare breasts again his back and began massaging that sinfully perfect part of his body he'd managed to entice me with for so very, very long.

You can run, but you can't hide. "You shall taunt me no more."

"Are you looking at my ass?" Paolo mumbled.

"Yes! Yes, I am. And it's even better than I imagined." Then again, so was the rest of him.

"And are those your gorgeous naked breasts pushed against my back."

"Yes. Yes, they are." I grinned, and then slid my hand from his naked, round backside to his front. My fingertips found exactly what I'd hoped for: a large, thick hard piece of Paolo. "Is that your penis?"

He turned over and rolled on top of me, pinning me underneath him. "Yes. And it wants to do very bad things to you."

The throbbing heat between my legs returned with a vengeance.

I smiled up at his beautiful stubble-framed lips. They were full and exotic and just as seductive as the rest of him.

"Such as?" I asked.

He raised his brows and grinned before reaching for another condom. Like the well-trained man that he was, he swiftly applied it and returned to me.

"I'm waiting," I said, "for a list of those bad things."

He began rubbing his steely-hard warmth over my sore but needy flesh. "I want to watch you moan with pleasure as I shamelessly fuck you."

"What? You dirty, dirty boy. I thought you loved me? Or is that how a big, scary man talks to a woman?"

He laughed. "Big and scary? Well, I am big."

"Yes, yes you are," I agreed cheerfully.

"And you should be scared. Because I like to fuck in the morning." He kissed me quickly. "I save the lovemaking for the afternoon and evenings."

I shrugged. "Sounds good to me."

His smiled melted away, and he looked at me with utter adoration. I felt his love, now that it wasn't hidden by a thick wall of scar tissue and guarded by the ghosts from his past. "I don't know what I would have done if anything happened to you."

I touched his beautiful lips with my fingertips. "Don't think about that. You saved me. We're together. End of story."

He bent his head and kissed me softly, but when his hips moved forward, the penetration was anything but gentle. He slid all the way in, sending a jolt of pleasure rocketing through my pelvis. I lifted my hips, driving him deeper.

"You're so beautiful," he said, pumping himself in a slow, steady rhythm. His one hand moved to my breast and kneaded gently. "And these are so perfect."

"Not as beautiful as that ass." I kissed him deeply and grabbed those two perfect mounds, savoring the way they flexed and hardened against my palms.

Feeling that familiar tension build rapidly, I urged him to move deeper and faster. His pace quickened, and he slammed his hips against mine, bringing me almost to the tipping point. He suddenly pulled out and flipped me onto my side.

"Not yet," he said.

He slid inside me from behind and began moving slowly, deliberately, pushing himself as deeply as my body would allow. I felt the tip of his shaft press against the most delicious spot, as if it were plucking the erotic chords of every female inch of me.

"Oh my God. What are you doing?" I panted.

"Fucking you."

No. He was doing so much more than that. I thought I might go insane with the relentlessly slow, exquisitely torturous pace. "God Paolo, please finish me off."

He ignored my request, his hips continuing to piston, and just when I thought I might scream from needing it so badly, he reached around and began massaging my swollen bud. My body instantly ignited, and I finally did scream. Paolo's loud, masculine groan followed.

After a few moments of lying there, catching our breath, Paolo withdrew and pulled me tightly to his body, wrapping his arms around me.

"Never again," he whispered.

I remember he'd said the same thing the night before.

"Never again what?" I asked.

"Let you go."

"I hope not," I murmured. Not after this. And, if for some reason we ever got separated, I could only pray he'd find me again.

"Wait. You never told me how you knew where I was," I said.

His eyes went wide, and he hopped from the bed, disappearing into the bathroom.

What the…? "Paolo?"

I heard him clear his throat. "We have our ways," he called out.

"Paolo, stop hiding and come here. What ways?"

Paolo appeared in the doorway with a white towel wrapped around his waist. The blissful, sated look on his face had evaporated. Now he just looked downright uncomfortable.

"Holy shit, Paolo," I sat up, "you guys didn't put some microchip in my head, did you?"

He scratched his forehead and came to sit beside me. "No."

"Then what? And why do I feel like I'm not going to like this."

"Because you won't," he said. "But remember, we did it for your own good. And it *did* save you."

I pulled the sheet up over my body and crossed my arms. "Tell me."

He sighed. "Hand me my phone."

I did, and he began tapping the surface. Then he showed me the screen.

"What the hell?" I said. It was a page from my notebook. "You guys copied my diary?"

My mind began to race with all of the crazy, stupid, and personal—yes, personal!—things I'd written in there.

I grabbed the phone and flipped through the screens. There were hundreds and hundreds of pages. My dreams of Paolo, my self-deprecating thoughts, and lots and lots of…just me, pining for Paolo.

"How embarrassing." I looked at him. "Both you and my father read this?"

He nodded.

"My most private thoughts." *I'm going to kill them.* "But how did you make copies?"

"We didn't," he replied. "The notebook is," he cleared his throat, "not really a notebook. It's made from a special material that only looks like paper. Everything you write

195

goes through a small, nearly undetectable transmitter that can't be tracked."

I wanted to punch him but was too mortified.

"Your father," he continued, "though I disagreed, thought it was the only way to really know what was going on in your life, who you were hanging out with." He smiled stiffly. "I'm sure he meant well."

I dropped my head. I couldn't believe it. I'd written down my very explicit dreams. Every detail. And come to think of it, that one morning when Paolo had arrived to take me to school, he'd been incredibly flustered.

"Wait. When you disappeared earlier this year, was it because of this?" I asked. Because I wouldn't blame him. I must've sounded like a depraved slut.

"Your father was not happy when he saw what you wrote," Paolo said. "Then you wished I'd go away because I was ruining your life, and he was more than happy to oblige. I was more than happy to get the hell out of there before you got me into trouble."

"So that's why you left?" I asked.

He nodded. "You have no idea how hard it was to keep my hands off you, Dakota. Especially after you wrote about us in the shower. I wanted you the moment I saw you, but after that, you made it fucking impossible. I haven't been able to take my mind off you since."

That makes two of us.

"I think," he added, "the fact you told you're mother about me—that you didn't know me—saved my ass. I wouldn't have lasted another day if she hadn't found out your father lied to her."

Lied? "About what?"

"That was her rule. She understands why he does what he does. I think she loves him for it. But her one condition was to keep you and her completely insulated. No bodyguards. No spying on you guys. She insisted you have a normal life."

That explained my mother's bizarre behavior once I told her the truth about Santiago.

"I can't believe this." I paused to digest for a moment. "But if she didn't know who you were right away, then why did she act like she knew you the day I got run over?"

"I lied to her." He flashed a guilty grin. "I told her you and I had been secretly dating for almost a year, but that you were afraid to tell her. She was extremely upset at you for not trusting her."

No wonder she never brought up anything about him. And no wonder she acted so pissed at the hospital that day. "Paolo! How could you?"

"I did what I had to."

"And when you came back to watch over me at college?" I asked, because by then she already knew who he was.

"I think she realized she couldn't protect you anymore. She asked your father to bring me back. Of course, he knew you were still...*into me*," he coughed.

Yes, I'd written about Paolo incessantly, like a girl with a bad teen idol crush. But it was only because my notebook was the only place I could turn to after Santiago slash Paolo had showed up and then mysteriously disappeared.

"You mean completely obsessed," I admitted pathetically.

"And that."

"You must've thought I was crazy," I said. "Because I sure the hell did."

"No, I didn't. Truthfully, I couldn't forget about you— your smart mouth, your fiery personality, your humility. You are the sexiest, most intriguing woman I've ever met. I jumped at the chance to see you again. It was all too convenient for me that your father's motives were to have me keep every guy on campus away from you. I would get you all to myself."

That bastard! And he'd made sure I had a brand-new notebook just waiting for me to pour my heart into on the first day of college.

"Don't be angry." Paolo brushed the hair from my shoulder and kissed me gently. "I was flattered that you dreamed about me so much. And that you thought I was a space alien. And a demon. And a ghost, asshole, chauvinistic pig."

Served him right.

I looked at my hands, thinking through how things must've looked from his point of view, knowing my secrets, pretending not to. *Ugh!* "You knew how I felt, but you let me keep making a fool of myself?"

"Have you ever read your journal?" he asked. "The only thing I knew was that you wished me dead and had very erotic dreams about me. A lot."

"Oh my God. This is so embarrassing. I will never write anything down ever again. Stupid notebook."

"That notebook saved your life," he said.

Paolo explained that everything I wrote while being held captive gave them all the clues they needed to find me: the description of being stuck with a needle, the fact I had been locked in a basement, how the person who took me was Mr. M—an insider with access to their communications.

"We knew," he said, "you were only a few hours away because you'd written about *waking up* in a basement. That meant sedatives. The kind our people use only last for an hour and a half to two at most. There aren't many houses with basements in that geography."

Once I'd written in my notebook that I'd been taken, my father had a hundred analysts, scouts, and "friends" searching every house I might be inside. Paolo was already on the tenth home when he saw me coming out with Mr. M.

"I've never wanted to kill anyone, Dakota," he said. "Never like this. But when I saw him handcuffing you, shoving you into that car, I could only imagine the things he'd done. When I shot him, it was the first time in my life I'd enjoyed it."

Oh. "Well, if it's any consolation, he was taking me to someone who was going to chop me into tiny bits and pieces. So, not sure I feel too bad about you shooting him."

Paolo looked at me and gave a little smile. "I didn't think I'd recover from my rage—not only at him, but at myself."

"You're a good man, don't ever doubt that," I said, knowing that my words fell seriously short compared to how I felt about him.

"So you forgive me for reading your diary?" he asked.

Hmmm. Did I? It was hard to be mad when that notebook had saved my life. A bizarre twist of fate. *My fate book.*

"I'm not angry. But my father is such a jerk!"

The cell on the nightstand began to vibrate. It was the same number as before.

"Speaking of, there he is now," Paolo said.

"Are you sure?" I asked.

He nodded.

"Let me answer—"

He snatched the phone from my hands. "Let me."

I understood that he wanted to shield me from the ugliness of the situation, but I had lots and lots to discuss with my father, ranging from the fact that he'd lied to me, manipulated me, spied on me, and threatened to kill the man I loved.

"Dane," Paolo said coldly. Several moments passed, and I saw the look on Paolo's face change. It was the first time I'd ever seen him look pale. "I see."

He held out the phone. "He wants to talk to you."

Great. Because the son of a bitch had this coming. I stood up from the bed and wrapped the sheet around my body before taking the phone. "Dad, I want you to know—"

"Do you love him, Dakota?" my father asked. No hello. No I'm sorry. Just…do you love him?

"What?" I asked, feeling confused.

"Do. You. Love. Him?" My father's tone was stern and bitter, like the time I'd driven my car into the neighbor's fence.

"Yes, more than anything. Where are you going with this? And where's Mom? Is she okay?"

"Dakota, Mr. McGregor did more than simply hunt you down and take you. He posted pictures of you and your mother on every Internet site out there. Every hit man, cartel boss, mobster, and enemy of the state now knows you exist and what you look like."

Oh shit. "What does that mean?" *Aside from very bad things?*

"It means that I'm retiring and going into hiding. Your mother is coming with me. Otherwise, I'd never see her again. I can't live with that, not after everything we've been through to stay together. You are both…my life."

My pulse ticked up a bit. I heard the sincerity in his voice, but his actions felt so wildly different. Words couldn't undo years of being pissed off. This was…

"Such a fucking mess."

"Dakota, I don't approve of that language," my father said. "We raised you better than that."

"Did *we* raise me? Really?" Why the hell was I bringing this up now? It felt so petty, given the situation. Yet, there I was, summoning my old ghosts. "Can I just talk to Mom?"

"We're not done yet," he said.

"Then say what you need to say."

He didn't respond immediately, and I almost thought he wouldn't, so I was about to let loose, but then he said, "Every day, every step, every success and failure I missed was because I had to. I can't tell you how sorry I am for not being there. However, life is never perfect, and I wouldn't change a thing. Not when so many lives survived because I made that sacrifice." The weight of his sorrow echoed in his breath. "But that's all water under the bridge now, Dakota. It's over. It's time for me to put you and your mother first. Your lives and your happiness."

As sad as the situation was, and as shady as my father might be, the fact that he'd give up everything to protect my mother and be with her, redeemed him in my eyes. Almost.

"Does she know about that woman?" I asked.

My father was silent for several moments. "The other woman was a decoy. A highly trained, highly paid, decoy wife who knew how to protect herself. I've always had one because she kept anyone from suspecting my real wife lived safely in the suburbs with little to no protection. Your mother always insisted on keeping things separate. Obviously, I lied to her and embedded people all around you two, but I've never been unfaithful to your mother. I would never hurt your mother like that. Or you. Your happiness is everything."

"Oh." Well, that sort of made me feel better. My father was a liar and shady, but not a cheater.

"This is why I'm letting you choose, Dakota. You can come with me and your mother—I planned for something like this to happen and can easily protect you both—or you can stay with Paolo."

Too shocked to stand, I sat back down on the bed, hugging the sheet to my body.

I was about to ask why we couldn't all go somewhere together, but that was stupid. My father would probably kick Paolo in the teeth the minute he saw him touch me.

In any case, my father had just told me that I could never go back to my old life, but somehow, I didn't care. After nearly dying multiple times in recent months, I knew what was important. It wasn't about looking to create an unattainable state of perfection sometime in the future. It was about living the life I had. Making the absolute most of every moment. The rest—how I'd finish school, where we'd live, how we'd stay out of sight—we'd have to figure out. But I wanted to live my life—my strange, strange life—with Paolo.

I sighed, knowing I'd miss my parents, especially my mother. "When will I see you again?" I asked, indirectly answering his question.

"When it's safe."

"How long?" I asked.

I heard the sadness in my father's voice. "Paolo has access to enough money to last three lifetimes, and he'll keep you safe."

It spoke volumes about Paolo that my father kept trusting him with my life, but…

"How long?" I asked again.

Long pause. "Maybe never, Dakota."

"Oh." Tears filled my eyes. I couldn't imagine never seeing them again.

Paolo slid his strong hand into mine and gazed at me with sympathy. He already knew what my father was telling me.

"Then I will pray every day that 'never' turns into just a few years." Yes, maybe things would die down after a while, and we'd find a way.

"I'll hope for the same, Dakota." There was a quick pause. "I have to hang up. I've been on this line too long. I love you. Everything I did was because of that."

"I know. I love you, too. And tell Mom I love her and miss her."

"I will."

"And, Dad?"

"Yes?"

"I lost my notebook, but if you figure out how to send me another one, I'll write every day. Okay?"

He chuckled softly. "I'd like that."

The call ended, and I handed Paolo back his phone. He quickly popped out the battery. I guessed it was to kill the signal.

"So you made your choice?" he asked.

I bobbed my head. "You."

He pulled me into his broad chest and stroked the back of my head. "I'm sorry you had to choose."

So was I, but strangely, I was happy, too. My mother finally got her wish: My father had quit his job, and she had him all to herself. As for me, my journey hadn't ended up where I'd wanted, but my ghost—made of solid flesh and bone, and who loved me—was all I wanted. I had faith that everything else would work itself out—I'd find a way to see my parents again.

"I don't know, seems like fate to me," I said.

He kissed me deeply and then stared into my eyes. "I love you."

"I love you, too.

He smiled awkwardly. "So are you ready?"

My stomach lurched. "Ready for…what?"

Paolo cupped my cheek. "We can't stay here. Not after so many phone calls—even with precautions, it's too risky."

"Where will we go?" I asked.

Paolo grinned and then shrugged. "I'm not sure, actually. Falling in love with you and running away was the one thing I never planned for."

How funny. Mr. Contingency didn't have one for this scenario? I found that completely adorable for some reason.

I gave it a moment of thought. "How about Italy?" He spoke the language.

His mouth twisted a bit. "About that, Dakota, I should tell you something."

Oh no.

Again, he smiled awkwardly. "Remember I told you about my family?"

"Powerful. Connected. Something like that?" I said, with dread in my tone.

"Yes," he said. "The reason I went to work for your father is because I wanted to escape them."

I gasped. "Whyyy?"

"They are not very nice people. Think, Godfather, but much worse."

Oh great. "Your family is…Italian mobsters?"

"They prefer to be called *la famiglia*, but yes. And my mother's death was just one of many in a long string of retaliations and tragedies. That's why I left as soon as I could. I couldn't be a part of that. Your father was the one who helped me escape them."

I felt a twinge of pride. He had to be a good guy, right? "Are they looking for you?" I asked.

"I think they've given up, but I'm not sure." That sounded like a story, an unpleasant one, for another day. And I'd kind of reached my limit.

I sighed. "Okay. Nix on Italy," I said. "How about somewhere warm in Latin America?" I assumed Paolo's Spanish was decent; he was great at faking the accent.

"Excellent choice." Paolo kissed me again, but then I had another thought.

"Wait. Is there anything else I need to know about you? Prison record? Wanted by the FBI?"

Funny. Paolo actually paused to think about the answer. "There is much to tell you, but nothing like that."

I sighed with relief.

"Come. It's time to get dressed." He took my hand and pulled me up from the bed, and stared into my eyes.

"Can I send Mandy and Bridget postcards before we go?"

"No. I'm sorry," he said. "But we will find another way to let them know you are all right."

Good. Because I wouldn't want them to worry.

I kissed him quickly. "Just promise that wherever we end up, I'll get a chance to study psychology, and that I can get my Spy Kids training. I have a feeling I'll need both."

"You do understand that you won't actually have to work? Ever," he added.

"If you think I'm going to sponge off you for the rest of my life—"

"You're more than welcome to; however, as much as I've earned over these past few years, I'm certain your father's investment skills far exceed mine."

What did he mean by that? "Sorry?"

"Dakota, your father made a very large sum of money over the years. And since your mother insisted on living like a normal, middle-class family, I don't think he spent much."

"And?" I asked.

"Let us just say that I'm a lowly, single-digit millionaire compared to you."

I sucked in a breath and let the air flap my lips. This news was simply one more strange, strange thing to pile on top. And, frankly, it didn't fall into the "critical" or "life-threatening" heap. *Nope. Don't care.*

"So you've been stalking me for my fortune?" I said jokingly.

"Of course. What other reason would I want you, other than for your vast fortune?" His eyes swept over my body.

"Funny."

"I have my moments," he said. But with his thick accent, which I'd now become accustomed to, it sounded like he'd said, *I hab my momenzzz.*

"So, given that money is no object, does that mean I can still go to school?" I asked.

He grinned proudly, and I wondered if it was because he liked the fact I wouldn't become a giant slacker.

"For you, anything is possible, Dakota."

I beamed at him. Because when a man like Paolo said something like that, you knew it had to be true. It was like he controlled the universe single-handedly. "Anything, huh?"

"Anything," he said confidently.

"Do we have time for a shower?"

His eyes lit with joy. "We'll have to make it fast, but I thought you'd never ask."

EPILOGUE

Undisclosed Location. Six Months Later…

"*Buenos días*, Julia. The usual?"

From the back of the line, I nodded at the tall barista in the white apron. "Gracias, Miguel! Can you add a café Americano to my order today?"

He nodded cheerfully. "*Por supuesto.*"

Miguel was also a student, so I always left him a nice tip, which is why he often started my order the moment he saw me—"Julie," a.k.a. "Julia"—walk through the door. I came daily to this beachside café because it had the best coffee in town and was only two blocks from our apartment. Okay, it wasn't exactly an apartment. More like a luxury villa for expats, with an ocean view. But who was asking? Thank God, no one. Paolo said it was better to hide in plain sight, playing the role of wealthy foreigners on an extended vacation, than to try to lie low in a shady part of town. Too suspicious, he'd said.

"Is he making my order? Or do I have to go to the back of the line?" I felt Paolo's thick, strong arms slip around my waist and his hot breath bathe the nape of my neck.

I sighed happily. "You're two minutes late. But would I forget your drink, *Santiago*?" I swiveled in his arms and gazed up at his deeply bronzed, beach town skin. I had to admit, the tropics did Paolo—alias Santiago—justice. Not long after we arrived here, I discovered he loved scuba diving, sailboarding, sailing, snorkeling, running, and swimming…He was a one-man decathlon. And, thankfully, a great instructor for all the stuff I didn't know how to do.

He gave me a long, deep, lazy kiss. "No, Julia. You always look after me," he said suggestively.

Oh boy. If he started, I wouldn't be able to resist him, and then we'd end up arrested for public fornication.

I turned back toward the register, mentally fanning my face. "You just like me because I'm your sugar mama."

He pinched my ass through my sundress, and I yelped.

"Hey! Just for that, you're paying for coffee." I kissed him and trotted outside to the sandy patio with the view of that turquoise water I couldn't get enough of. California beaches were nothing like this.

I made a little playful wave at Paolo—who looked delicious in his wrinkled, white linen shirt and well-loved cutoffs—through the window and sat down at my favorite small table. It was the one with the giant umbrella, right next to the tall coconut tree. My pale skin and I needed lots of shade.

I began digging out my books, running verb conjugations through my head. I was taking only Spanish classes for now, but next semester, after I got the language down, I planned to take courses in psychology.

I slipped my binder from my backpack and saw a large manila envelope wedged inside.

Oh my God. It couldn't be. Feeling giddy, I tore open the envelope and slid out its contents.

Yes! There was a new notebook and folded letter.

"Ah, I see you found your surprise." Paolo—errr—Santiago—whatever—walked toward me with two cups of coffee. A small breeze blew his sun-streaked hair over his eyes, and he made a little huff with his breath to clear his view.

So cute. So sexy. I was so in love with this man.

"But h…h…how?" I asked.

He smiled with those gorgeous, stubble-framed lips and set the coffee in front of me. "I have my ways." He glanced at the letter in my hand. "Read it."

I unfolded the white paper, immediately recognizing my mother's handwriting. My heart lifted. Over the past few months, I'd come to accept everything that had happened. I felt happier than ever, actually. But my biggest regret was not being able to say good-bye to my mom or talk to her every day.

My eyes quickly scanned the paper and drank in the words. "They're somewhere cold," I mumbled to Paolo, who sipped his coffee with a triumphant grin. He knew he'd "done good."

"And," I added, "she says she's enjoying having my father all to herself for once, although he snores now, and it keeps her up a lot."

"Keep reading," he said.

But as happy as I am, Dakota, to be with your father, to be healthy and alive, I miss you. More than I could ever say in this letter. Which is why I told your father that he is a giant ass for not finding a way for us all to be together. For heaven's sake, the man stopped a nuclear attack on the United States, but he can't figure out how to let me see my only daughter? Well, you can imagine that I wasn't having it. Which is why by the time you get this letter I'll be right there to read it with you.

"Huh?" I looked up at Paolo, whose grin was almost as wide as my eyes.

"Right behind you," he said.

I jumped from the chair and found my mother's warm smile and big blue eyes. "Surprise, baby."

"Oh my God." We hugged tightly, and I couldn't help but cry. I pulled away and looked at her smiling face, unable to really believe she was standing there. "But how? Is it safe?"

"Not to worry, Dakota, your father and I were very careful. But we won't be staying long. Just a few days."

I didn't care. I was happy to see her, no matter for how many minutes, hours, days—whatever.

"Where's Dad?" I asked.

She chuckled and pointed to a man about a hundred yards down the beach, standing under a tree. He wore a straw hat, dark sunglasses, and a blue Hawaiian shirt. I could tell from the way he stood that his eyes were scanning everything in the vicinity. I'd seen Paolo do it a thousand times.

My mother shrugged. "He's a little paranoid. Just let him do his thing; I'm sure he'll be over in a minute." She looked at Paolo. "Oh, sorry." She gave him a warm hug. "I can't thank you enough for helping to arrange this, *Santiago*." She said his name with a deliberate emphasis as if to tease him.

He bowed his head. "It's my pleasure. Anything to make *Julie* happy."

My mother looked back at me, beaming. "Julie. It's a great name. And you look just," she sighed, "gorgeous. The most beautiful bride-to-be ever."

"Bride?" I asked.

Paolo cleared his throat, and my mother covered her mouth. "Oops. I just ruined the surprise, didn't I?"

I looked at Paolo, then my mother, and then back again at him. "What's she talking about?"

"I'll just be right over there with your father." My mother scurried away, with a goofy grin.

"Paolo?"

He stepped in and slid his arms around my waist. "I was going to propose tonight during dinner."

Marriage. He wanted to marry me. I can't say that the thought hadn't crossed my mind, but I figured we would make that leap when the time came and things settled down and I was done with school and we had a house and...*Crap. There I go again. Waiting for everything to be perfect. Idiot.*

Of course I'd marry him. I couldn't imagine life without the man. Having a house, job, and degree wouldn't change that.

"I love you, Dakota. You're everything to me." Paolo's voice was deep and sincere. "So, what do you say?" he pulled a small black box from his pocket. His dark eyes glowed with happiness and his usual confidence, which made me wonder.

"By any chance, did you plan a wedding for tomorrow?" I asked.

"No. Your mother insisted we give you a real wedding, which she insists on planning."

I assumed there wouldn't be anyone there except us four, but I loved the idea of having a proper dress, cake, ceremony…It was perfect. I had everything I ever hoped for.

I pushed up onto my tiptoes to reach his lips and gave him a quick kiss. "I'll think about." I wanted to see him squirm. Just a little.

He chuckled. "You'll *think* about it?"

I grabbed my stuff and began walking toward my parents. "Yeah," I called out. "I also want to make sure my dad doesn't still plan on killing you."

"That's not funny," he replied.

He ran up behind me and grabbed me by the waist. Our feet got all tangled, and I fell into the warm sand. Paolo came crashing on top of me.

I rolled over and Paolo sat on top of me, pinning me down. "Say yes or I'm not letting you go."

"Are you insane? My parents are watching." I expected my father would appear at any moment and kick the crap out of him.

Paolo glanced happily in their direction. "Let them watch. I'm not letting you up until you say yes."

"Oh my god. You're crazy. Yes. Yes! I'll marry you. Just get off me."

He grinned and pecked me on the lips. "Anything for you."

THE END

৵৵

Note From the Author:

Hi, All! I hope you enjoyed my first non-paranormal, non-cliffhanger novel! If you did, please let me know! Click those happy little stars on the e-tailer's website or write a review (I read the helpful ones, but not the ones posted by mean people, because mean people suck!), shoot me a note, or stalk me on Facebook or Twitter. I also have a Goodreads Ask Mimi Group where you'll find many goodies for my readers and steamy, fun, sometimes strange conversations and giveaways. Contact info is below!

Happy Reading!
Mimi

Extras and Contact Info

Want to see images of Santiago/Paolo, Dakota, or places from the story?

Go to: http://www.mimijean.net/fate_book.html

Find out about new releases, check out the *New York Times* and *USA Today* best-selling Accidentally Yours series, subscribe to Mimi's mailing list, or contact her online:

http://www.mimijean.net
http://twitter.com/MimiJeanRomance
https://www.facebook.com/MimiJeanPamfiloff
http://www.goodreads.com/group/show/101923-ask-mimi-jean-pamfiloff
mailto:mimi@mimijean.net

About the Author

Before taking up a permanent residence in the San Francisco Bay Area, Mimi spent time living near NYC (became a shopaholic), in Mexico City (developed a taste for very spicy food), and Arizona (now hates jumping chollas but pines for sherbet sunsets). Her love of pre-Hispanic culture, big cities, and romance inspires her to write when she's not busy with kids, hubby, work, and life...or getting sucked into a juicy novel. Or hosting the Man Candy Show on Radioslot.com! (Be very afraid!)

She hopes that someday leather pants for men will make a big comeback, and that her writing might make you laugh (or give you a mini-vacay) when you need it most.

30116206R00125

Made in the USA
San Bernardino, CA
05 February 2016